Broken

Broken

WILLOW WINTERS

If you'd like me to let you know as soon as my books are released as well as other fantastic promotions, sign up for my bad boy mailing list here: http://eepurl.com/b2izzf

Get a FREE book when you sign up!

If you'd be interested in getting my latest books for FREE (and before release!) in exchange for an honest review, you can also sign up for my Advance Review Copy Team mailing list here: http://eepurl.com/b3jNnP

You can check out my Facebook page here for sneak peeks at upcoming books, giveaways, or just to send a message to my Facebook profile, Willow Winters

And check out my Begging for Bad Boys Facebook group for ARC invitations, Freebies and New Releases from your favorite Bad Boy Romance authors.

Or, if all else fails, I check my email often! You can get a hold of me anytime at:
badboys@willowwinterswrites.com

Onto the bad boys... Enjoy!

Heartless. Ruthless. Stone Cold Killer.

That's me. I destroy anything in my path to get what I want.

Then she showed up. Olivia Bell. She's sweet and innocent, and in the wrong place, at the wrong time.

Now she's mine. *My property.* I *own* her. Given to me as a bargaining chip.

She's not a part of my plans, but plans change. Her pouty lips and gorgeous curves beg me to break her.

Taking her lush curvy body, and ravaging it for all its worth would be easy, but I want to earn her submission. It's addictive. I want it. I want *her*.

They wanted me to break her. I am. And I'm enjoying it. Now they want to take her from me.

Over my dead body.

Let them come for us. I'll kill them all.

By the time I'm done, everyone will know. *She belongs to me.*

This is a DARK romance. A full-length standalone novel with HEA and no cheating

Contents

PROLOGUE

Olivia

THE COURTROOM IS QUIET. I CAN HEAR SOMEONE in the back of the room clear their throat. I swallow thickly and try to avoid their gazes. But I'm on the witness stand, I can't avoid them or any of this.

They're all watching me. Waiting for an answer. I feel like I'm suffocating. This is too much.

It reminds me of being in the room with him. With Kade. My eyes dart to him, and my mouth parts slightly as I remember the time I spent with him.

The other men would watch. He said I had to be perfect, and if I was he'd give me my freedom. And he did. He's a man of his word. But this freedom feels empty and hollow. I wish I could take it back. Not our time together, just my wish to be set free.

"Miss Bell?" asks the prosecution, snapping me out of my reverie.

"Yes?" I ask warily. My fingers twist in my hand. My heartbeat picks up. I don't want to be here. I'd give anything to go back.

They're waiting for me to talk, to testify against him and give evidence that Kade's a bad man. That he deserves to be imprisoned not only for what he did to me, but for everything else.

But I can't. He did it to protect me. He *had* to do it. My voice is caught in my throat. My blood heats and chills at the same time. The thought of turning against him makes me sick.

My eyes focus on him, and all I want to do is to run to his side. I wish he could just take me away. Instead he's on trial, and I'm left alone to deal with the aftermath of how my life has changed forever.

Tears prick my eyes as Kade nods his head and gives me a small, sad smile. He wants me to answer them. He wants me to be a good girl and tell them everything they want to know so I can go free. *It's time to let go, angel.* I hear his words and I hate them. I don't want to let go of him. I was his, and now I feel like I'm no one.

"Do you need me to repeat the question?" the old man says as he stares at me through his spectacles.

I shake my head. I know what he asked. I know what they want from me.

My body relaxes as I remember how he broke me down bit by bit. Now it seems calculated, as though he knew what he was doing. Like he used me. That's what they keep telling me, they say that's why I feel this way about him. But back then, it felt different. It felt as though he was helping me. I thought he needed me. *He did need me.*

His fingers gently slid down the curve of my hip. *"My angel,"* he whispered. His lips barely touched the shell of my ear, his hot breath sending chills down my shoulder. As his hand slid farther down, he groaned with satisfaction. I was always ready for him. I learned to love what he did. I learned to be perfect for him.

"Miss Bell, answer the question." The judge's voice rings out and makes my body jolt in the seat.

I clear my throat thinking about where I should start and what all I should tell them. My heart clenches in my chest. I don't want to share it with them. Right now these memories are mine. They'll ruin them. They'll make me think my recollections are something they aren't.

They want me to believe he never loved me, and that the feelings I have for him are false.

I don't know what to do. I don't know what to believe.

The only thing I know that's true is I fell in love with Kade and that now, because of him, I'm utterly and completely broken.

CHAPTER 1

Olivia

Three months earlier...

I FEEL SICK TO MY STOMACH. I WISH I COULD just throw up and be done with this feeling, but it's not from drinking too much, or food poisoning, or anything like that. I'm just sick of my life and the shitty position I put myself in. Getting turned down for your ninth job interview sucks. And it was for a hair salon. Like, really? All I'd be doing is bookwork. It can't be that fucking hard. I'm starting to think there's no hope. That's what makes me so damn sick. Like there's nothing I can do, and I'm just screwed.

It's been three weeks since I got expelled from the university. It was all over alcohol. They have a zero tolerance policy. So of course getting kicked out also meant losing my scholarships. And losing my scholarships meant losing my income, plus my part-time job in the registrar's office. Which means when the rent is due, I'm fucked if I can't hurry up and land a job already.

As if this wasn't already the worst month of my life, my mother won't even answer my calls. It's her idea of tough love. Yeah, I know I fucked up. I don't need to hear it again. It's not like this is what I usually do. Like I went to college and suddenly became a horrible person. I was in all the honors classes in high school. I was a teacher's pet.

I've gotten straight A's my entire life, except for that one C in Advanced Literature. Fuck English, I only took the class because I had to in order to fulfill my graduation requirements.

I've always been a brown-noser, as Cheryl calls me.

Fuck, Cheryl. It's her fault!

I bite my lip and cross my arms over my chest to warm myself up. I shake my head, trying not to be bitter about it all. It's not really Cheryl's fault. She may have put the bottle in my hand, but she didn't make me drink. She was only trying to help. After all, it's not every day that your first real boyfriend, the man you gave your virginity to, dumps you for someone prettier.

Tears prick my eyes, but I'm sure as shit not going to cry over him. I'll cry over my self-esteem though, because that shit hurt. When I asked him how he could just break up with me like our relationship meant nothing to him, he just shrugged and said her tits were bigger. Fucking asshole. How did I ever fall for him?

Daniel Croast is hot and athletic, and really knows how to lay on the charm.

But he's a fucking dick. I knew this, yet I still fell for him. I still spread my legs for him and let him take every last piece of me that he wanted.

Curse my fucking hormones. Tall, with broad shoulders. He played on the rugby team and there's just something about men crashing into each other and taking those brutal hits; it makes my pussy pulse with desire. I'm not a biology major, but it was definitely my fucked-up hormones.

I fell in lust, not love.

I finally had a boyfriend and friends. Real friends who liked me for me. Cheryl may be a bad influence and not have a clue about how the real world works, but deep down I know she cares about me. Drinking on campus in the dorms was stupid though.

Real fucking stupid. I just went there to cry to Audrey about everything, and instead we ended up drinking. I even thought, *No, we should go to our apartment if we're going to be drinking*. Shit, that's the entire reason we got the apartment off-campus.

But I felt horrible, and my friends were all around me, and I just wanted to feel better.

I fucking hate that RA prick that busted us. I swear he's got a stick shoved up his ass. He can go to hell for all I care.

I turn twenty-one in two months, and Cheryl in three. That RA's so fucking pretentious and likes to pretend he did this for the "right reasons" but seriously, he can go fuck himself. He's never liked Audrey since she turned his scrawny ass down during freshman orientation. That's really what it was about, his dumb fucking vendetta.

Luckily for Audrey, she left to go get more booze. And while she was walking to the liquor store, campus security showed up. She got a strike, and we got booted.

So now I'm at the lowest point in my life.

What kills me the most is that my parents aren't talking to me, which I don't understand. I know they're disappointed and all, but the silent treatment is just not helpful. All it's doing is hurting me. I stop at the edge of the sidewalk and wait, standing in the chill of the fall night, hugging my arms tighter around myself. My legs are freezing since I wore a black A-line skirt to my interview, but at least I grabbed my cream chenille sweater.

I stare up at the red hand on the crosswalk sign and just wait.

There aren't any cars this late at night. But the hand is red. And that means you can't go, so I don't. I'm not a fan of breaking the rules.

I huff a laugh at this train of thought. The one time in my entire life I break the rules, and of course I get caught. And now everything I've worked so damn hard for is crumbling all around me. Tears prick at my eyes again, and this time one escapes.

I breathe out slow and steady, calming myself. I wipe the stray tear with the cuff of my sweater and start walking as soon as I get the green signal to go. Mascara covers the end of my sleeve now, but I don't care.

I feel like I'm balanced on the edge of a razor. One one side, I care entirely too much about everything, and my heart aches with all the disappointment I've caused, not to mention the disappointment I feel in myself. But on the other side, I don't give a fuck about any of this. I've hardened my heart with hate for everyone around me that doesn't care enough to try to help.

I swallow thickly. They don't have to help me. No one owes me anything, and that's just fine by me. I have a plan.

This isn't going to ruin me.

Yes, I got kicked out of one of the most prestigious

universities in the country, but I can get into another. If I can just get a job, I can survive until February for sure. That's when I'll find out if I got in anywhere else. I'm sure another school will take me. They can't hold having a drink over my head forever, especially since I'm sure this kind of thing happens all the time. I'm just happy they decided not to press charges, and it's not on my legal record. As for my academic record, it was embarrassing as hell to have to explain that I got kicked out for drinking on campus. But I'll do whatever I have to do.

I've already filled out twenty applications for other colleges. I filled out nearly forty for jobs.

I'll keep applying myself until someone gives me a break. I'm sure my professors are disappointed, but at least they were kind enough to offer their recommendations.

My heart twists in my chest. I hate disappointing people. Especially those I look up to. In my mind, I see Dr. Griffins shake her head slightly, mouth parted in shock as I told her I had to leave.

Disappointed.

Well, you and me both, I guess.

I keep walking down the sidewalk and I start to get a real uneasy feeling creeping over me. It's so fucking quiet. There's no one around. It's just dead. I'm pretty used to walking everywhere, even late at night, but not on this side of town. I don't even know what time it is.

I should be home this late at night. I shouldn't be here. It's obvious this isn't the safest part of town. But I just couldn't go back to the apartment and have nothing to tell Cheryl.

I'm the one who looks out for her. But right now I've got nothing for either of us.

I couldn't tell Cheryl that I didn't get the job, and that I have no plan for us.

She's freaking out about money. She's kind of a wild child, and she's never had a worry in her life. I love her free spirit and all, but that needs to take a back seat when your parents cut you off. She isn't like me though. She's never worked a day in her life. Between all my savings and the scholarships, I was able to pay for college on my own. Not Cheryl Fletcher. I don't think her perfectly manicured hands have ever performed any sort of manual labor. Which is fine if you don't have to, and it's not like she's a spoiled brat who throws it in your face.

But her parents were pissed about the expulsion and completely cut her off. And it's not like she isn't trying— she's filled out more job applications than I have. Partly because she doesn't plan on going back to school. She was undeclared anyway since she doesn't know what she wants to do with her life.

But the best plan we have to make rent this month is to start selling our shit. And by our shit, I mean hers. A purse or two from her collection would be enough to do it. I'm not going to ask though. My everyday purse is a clutch I bought on clearance from Target a few semesters ago. Hardly glamorous, and hardly expensive. Nope, not like Cheryl's newest purse, a Michael Kors hobo with buttery soft leather. Still, I'm not going to ask and put her in that position.

It's the only option I can think of though.

I see a few guys walking two blocks up from me. They're on the opposite side of the street and heading in my direction. I don't like it. They're talking and laughing, and having a good time. They don't seem threatening. But still, a young girl walking alone and three men... I just don't like it.

There's an alleyway on my left that lets out a few blocks down from the main road where our apartment is. As I stand in the opening, I can see it opens up on both walls of the alley halfway through and that there are some cars farther down on the other side. It's empty.

I don't even hesitate to take the left turn and walk toward more people. Toward safety. I'm pretty sure it's an even faster route home—I think, anyway.

It's dark, and things look different when it's dark.

I pick up my pace with my eyes straight ahead on the light at the opening to the other street.

I'm about halfway through, right near the openings on both sides of the alley when I hear shouting.

My heart jumps in my chest, and my breathing stalls. I

instinctively take a step back and nearly fall on my ass with fear.

It's *angry* shouting. More than two men arguing in what I think is Russian. Or maybe German. I don't know. All I know is that I don't understand anything they're saying, and I shouldn't be here. I look behind me for a moment, but I don't know where those three men are. Fuck. Fuck.

I don't know what to do. The yelling gets louder and closer. My heart hammers faster in my chest. I feel lost and trapped as my throat closes with fear.

I could just run as fast as I can through the opening. It's large enough that a car could get through. But they sound so close. If they saw me, they'd definitely be able to catch me before I made it out the other side.

I take a deep breath and chance a look, just a small glance to see what's happening.

My breathing slows, and the only thing I can hear is my blood rushing in my ears. My heart *thumps*, *thumps*, *thumps* way too loud. They're going to hear me; they're going to see me.

I feel a small sense of relief as I see a row of trashcans blocking the path. I can see past them though. Maybe twenty feet from me, there's a group of men gathered in the parking lot of a warehouse.

I don't know what's going on, but it's not good. So far, no one's spotted me since I'm peeking around the corner with just part of my head showing. I could still get down on the ground, try crawling in the dirt and gravel, and hope I get through unnoticed.

Instead I watch, paralyzed with disbelief at what I'm seeing.

A man's standing apart from the others. It's not the fact that he's in a custom-tailored suit when they rest of them are all in wrinkled khakis or worn-out jeans. He's one of the tallest men, with broad shoulders that stretches the rich fabric tight across his gorgeous frame. But that's not it either. His very presence is a dominating force. It's the air around him.

He's a dangerous man. The other men may be mean, or even pure evil. But this man is ruthless, calculated, and something tells me he can get away with it. He's a man who isn't denied, and for good reasons. The shadows on his face only make his high and sharp cheekbones even more severe. A light dusting of rough stubble lines his hard jaw.

He's handsome in the most sinful ways, but he'd break you without thinking twice. Maybe even intentionally.

He straightens his crisp white shirt from under his dark navy suit with a gun still firmly in his hand, his finger on the trigger. His barely contained anger is evident even at this distance. He's listening to the man screaming, the one being dragged over on his knees to the center where the other men are circling.

Another man, Ricky, is yelling back. At least I think that's his name, since that's what it sounds like they're calling him. Ricky is obviously in charge of the group of men who are mostly dressed in dark denim jeans, and Henleys or hoodies.

All but *him*.

All of them are under Ricky's control, except the man with the absolute power.

Their guns are pointed at the one man who's unarmed and on his knees. Two men are pushing down on his shoulders, forcing him to maintain that position.

"Fuck you! Fuck all of you!" the man on his knees yells out and spits on the ground.

"So it's true!" yells one of the men holding him down.

"Fucking pig! Fucking liar!" the men are yelling, practically chanting. I realize with a start that the man being forced to kneel must be an undercover cop. I fumble in my clutch for my phone. I need to get help.

"What did you tell them?" asks Ricky. *Bang!* I almost scream and have to cover my mouth with my hands as the sound of a bullet cries out and echoes through the alley. My phone drops to the ground, and the screen cracks from the impact.

My heart stills as Ricky yells out and grabs the cop's shoulder.

Somehow I don't think they heard me, or saw me. Their

focus is on the cop who's still on his knees clutching his leg and wincing in pain.

"The next one will be in your skull." Ricky walks closer to the man and puts the gun up to his temple, twisting the barrel of the gun to taunt him. "What did you tell them?"

The kneeling man attempts to laugh although he's in obvious pain. "Just do it. You'll never get anything from me." He sneers as blood soaks through his jeans. It's so dark, it almost looks black.

No! No! I need to do something. As I bend down to get my cracked phone, the man in the dark suit moves forward. A hush falls over the men. The only exception is Ricky, who's cussing and making threats that don't seem to affect the undercover cop.

"Is it true?" a deep, rich voice asks so calmly that it doesn't seem real. The loud click of his gun cocking makes me take a step forward. My head shakes. No. No.

It's silent. Everyone's waiting for his answer, even Ricky.

"Fuck you, you fucking criminal."

"What did you call me?" The man's voice raises with a deadly tone. He points his gun at his target's head.

"You really going to make me say it again?" the man on his knees asks, but his voice cracks. The fear of imminent death is finally coming through.

And with that, his death sentence is complete. One shot, *bang*, and he falls to the ground. The man in the suit moves his arm again and aims at the ground this time. I can't see, but I hear the shots ring out, again and again. *Bang, bang, bang!*

I shake my head with disbelief, tears leaking from the corners of my eyes. They killed him, and I saw the whole thing. My blood runs cold, and the sickness I'm feeling threatens to come up my throat.

And then I do scream. I shriek louder than I ever have before.

A pair of hard, unforgiving arms wrap around my waist and chest before a hand covers my mouth. I struggle against what feels like an unmoving brick frame holding me tight, my back to his hard chest. Caught. I've been caught. I fight for my life; my nails dig into his skin, piercing and scratching. But it does nothing. He's so much taller than I am, so he easily picks my body up off the ground and wraps his hand around my throat, suffocating me. I struggle as much as I can. But it's hopeless, I'm already losing consciousness. The last thing I see, before my world goes black, is the man in the suit looking down the alley. His intense gaze is focused solely on me.

CHAPTER 2

Olivia

I WAKE WITH PAIN RADIATING IN MY SHOULDER.
My throat feels bruised, and my head throbs with an unrelenting ache in my temples. Zip ties dig into the flesh of my ankles and wrists. They're so tight it feels like every move against them, no matter how small, cuts my skin.

My heart skips a beat, and I struggle not to open my eyes as I realize what's happened. I've been taken. I register I'm not alone when I hear voices. I need to be still. I need to be quiet. I need to get the fuck out of here. I can't risk drawing unnecessary attention to myself until I can figure a way out of this.

"Who let him in, Ricky?" I recognize his voice immediately, the voice of the man with power. The dangerous man from earlier, the man in the suit, and right now he sounds pissed. The sound of his anger alone is enough to paralyze my body.

"It's a mistake anyone could have made, Kade." Ricky's words are hard. The man in the suit might be in charge, but it's clear Ricky is as well.

"It's a mistake that could have ruined me."

"You never made more than a handful of contacts. He would've had nothing on you," Ricky says dismissively.

"It's unacceptable." Kade's words are sharp, and nearly make me jump. But I'm too scared to move. I have to remind myself to breathe as I begin to feel lightheaded.

"Well, we found out before anything got leaked," Ricky grumbles.

"Are you sure?" Kade asks.

"We're positive." I gather my courage, and slowly open my eyes to find myself in a cramped and dirty office. It's really small with drop ceiling tiles covered in dust and a flat wood laminate door.

Kade's sharp blue eyes are narrowed and hard. He obviously doesn't belong in this cramped, dirty office. There are cardboard boxes stacked in the corners, and a dirty old chair behind what looks to be an even older desk. Nothing in here is expensive. It's cheap and filthy. The other men belong here. But the man in the suit doesn't. He's as out of place as I am.

Two other men are seated in the far corner, while Kade and Ricky are standing in front of the desk to my left. Ricky leans against the cheap desk piled high with papers and folders, feigning a casual position. But the air is tense around the two men.

Ricky yells sharply at the men in the corner. It's something in Russian, definitely Russian. The only word I understand though is a name, Vic. The two men shake their heads, but only one replies. Of the two, he's taller and more built. His voice is deep, and he has a thick accent. After watching their exchange, I'm assuming he's Vic.

It's obvious they're obedient lap dogs. Now that I look at them more closely, I can see that both of the men in the corner are young. The short and pale one could be eighteen or younger. The other, Vic, is maybe in his early twenties. Vic looks deadly though. If you saw him walking down the street toward you, you'd run in the opposite direction. He looks like he'd love to take his anger out on someone. He probably does. He has a toothpick in the corner of his mouth, and he keeps looking at my body like he wants to be alone with me. Inwardly I shudder.

I need to get the fuck out of here.

Ricky responds to Vic with rapid-fire Russian, and somehow he seems even angrier than before. I don't want to make myself a target for that anger, but I can't help staring at Ricky during his tirade. His face is sunken in, and he has dark bags under his eyes. They don't look like the kind you get from lack of sleep though, more like the kind that come with age and alcohol.

Vic's eyes bore into me. He ignores his boss and looks intently past both men at me. I can feel his hatred. Whatever happens, I cannot be left alone with him.

Kade and Ricky continue to argue and Kade takes a step forward, blocking Vic from my sight. I heave in a breath I didn't know I was holding and try tugging uselessly on the zip ties binding my wrists. I wince as they bite into my skin.

It's useless.

As the weight of my situation starts to suffocate me, I feel Kade's piercing stare. My body trembles, and I slowly move my eyes to meet his. Somehow I already knew they were on me.

I'm struck by his masculine beauty. To say he looks like a sex god and CEO wrapped into one would be an understatement. But there's more. There's an edge of danger that's undeniable. His frame is domineering—tall, with broad shoulders and narrow hips. But it's his expression that's the most intimidating. My eyes sweep over him from his dark hair and piercing blue eyes, to his plush lips, slightly downturned with disapproval.

My eyes lift to meet his again, and I'm entrapped. As much as I want to look away, I'm forced to stare back.

My shoulders hunch inward with fear, and I feel like I can't breathe. It's as though he's choking me.

"And what of her?" Kade asks with his eyes still firmly on me. "His partner?" My eyes widen and I try to shake my head to deny it, but I can't. I'm paralyzed.

"No, just a dumb bitch," Ricky says scornfully. Kade whips his head around to face him. Kade takes a step forward and the two men cower slightly, shifting in their seats. Vic attempts to right himself, but it's obvious he feels threatened. Ricky stands his ground, but I swear I see a flash of fear cross his eyes.

"Tell me you did a background check on her?" He speaks slowly, and with menace dripping from his voice. "'Just a dumb bitch' isn't good enough."

Ricky keeps his gaze on Kade and gestures behind him toward the two men in the corner. The younger one looks to Vic with worry evident on his pallid face. Vic starts to respond in his heavily-accented English, "It's in—"

"Fucking get it!" Ricky snaps, causing the younger lackey to jump up and scurry from the room. Vic doesn't move, but he averts his eyes from Ricky and stares fixedly at the door where the other man went through.

Ricky's sallow skin turns red with anger as his veins swell in his neck. As explosive as his anger is, Kade's the one that scares me more. I don't think Ricky would appreciate the comparison though.

"Doesn't matter who she is." Ricky looks at me with a crooked smile exposing his yellowed teeth. "We're sending her with you." He looks back at Kade with a wicked glint in his eyes.

If he's trying to get a rise out of Kade with that comment, it's not happening. I look to Kade to gauge his reaction, and he's completely expressionless. It's clear he's utterly disinterested.

My body shakes harder, and I open my mouth to speak. "I—" "I—" I try to speak, but my throat is so dry. It croaks, and I stutter. I shake my head. My blood seems to boil, and my breath falls short. Heat overwhelms me.

"You—you—you—what?!" Ricky yells, and I instinctively jolt back. I scoot backward on my ass, my hands awkwardly and painfully dragging on the dirty linoleum floor until I feel my back against the wall. A sharp pain shoots through my shoulders and ankles. I can barely move with the zip ties holding me hostage. My heart beats chaotically, and it's only then that I realize I'm crying.

"She's not even trained," Kade sneers. I don't know what he means by that, but for some reason his disapproval of me hurts. My chest aches, and my face falls with sadness. Please, please don't leave me here with them.

His anger may scare me, but I feel as though I'd be safer with Kade.

"That's for you to do. You're supposed to be an expert

in this field, yet we've never seen your work," Ricky says as he leans against the desk once again and crosses his arms. Kade shoots him one arrogant, icy look before he speaks.

"For a good fucking reason. If I'd worked with Barrow like you pushed me to, I would've been fucked."

"Well you weren't," Ricky says as he dares to take a step forward, closer to Kade. Kade doesn't budge. "And now I'm not feeling very trusting of anyone."

Kade tilts his head and cocks a small but threatening grin. "You expect me to accept her, train her and show her off to you? When for all I know, she's a fucking cop!" Kade's shoulders lean forward with the last words.

Ricky's eyes turn cold and it's clear he's not shy about his hatred for Kade. "She's not a cop. We have her license and paperwork done. I'm sure of it." I want to speak; I want to plead with them to let me go. But I'm frozen with fear, my eyes darting between the two of them. "She goes with you, or she gets shipped off."

I break into a cold sweat, and I have to force myself to keep breathing when I hear what Ricky says. That option can't happen. I don't want to get *shipped off*, because what-ever the fuck that means, it's not good. It can't be good. "If you don't take her, you can take another. I don't give a fuck, but it's time we see what you can do."

Kade turns away from Ricky and looks at me for a moment before walking forward. I've still got my back up against the wall. My arms and wrists ache from being held behind me with zip ties. I can feel a trickle of blood from the plastic cutting into my skin.

My skirt has ridden up and my pale thighs are exposed. With my ankles bound, I'm trapped.

He crouches in front of me and seems to inspect every inch of me. He licks his lips as his eyes travel down my body. His masculine smell fills my lungs.

"Please," I beg in a whisper. "I won't tell anyone."

Ricky smiles wickedly at my words. He moves to the door as the man from earlier finally comes back. He hands a yellow folder to Ricky. "That's what they all say." He mimics my voice and mockingly says, "I won't tell a soul." Ricky, Vic, and the pale toady laugh, and all hope leaves me as hot tears fall down my cheeks.

Kade doesn't laugh, instead he continues to watch me. I lick my dry lips and try to wipe away my tears by brushing my face against my shoulder. I want to plead with him to take me away from them, but when I look up at him, there's no sympathy there. Only hard and cold blue eyes seemingly made of ice. My head falls to my chest, and I wish I could disappear.

"So, what will it be?" Ricky asks, drawing Kade's attention from me. He rises and walks away from me and I find myself trying to crawl toward him. I can't stay here. Not with Vic looking at me like a predator and the threat of being *shipped off*.

Kade grabs the folder from Ricky and opens it. I don't

know what's in there, but whatever he's looking for, I hope he finds it. I watch as his eyes travel down the page and then the next. Suddenly, he looks back at me with an expression of dissatisfaction.

"You're on birth control?" he asks.

My cheeks flame. I swallow the spiked lump in my throat and try to verbalize an answer, but I can't, so I nod my head.

They must have my school records. I just went to the gyno on campus a few months ago, after I decided to give myself to Daniel. I went with the shot because it seemed easier than having to remember to take a pill every damn day. I almost didn't get the last injection since we broke up, but I went and got it since I'd scheduled the appointment.

He shuts the folder and shoves it against Vic's chest.

He looks at Ricky and then back at me. I can't read his expression. I don't know what he's going to do or say, so I do the only thing I can do at this point. I wait with bated breath.

"After today, I could use a distraction." Kade turns back to Ricky and nods once as he says, "I'll take her. And then you give me what I want."

Ricky's lips pull into a wide smile and he says, "Deal."

CHAPTER 3

Olivia

MY THROAT'S HOARSE FROM SCREAMING through the gag, and I'm getting tired. I'm starting to really feel the exhaustion weighing down on me, but fear is keeping me wide awake.

I've tried to kick the trunk open to no avail. I've been kicking this entire time, hoping that maybe someone would see the thumping. It's not really kicking though since my ankles are bound. So I'm pushing all my weight to my chest and thrusting my legs upward. It hurts. The zip ties rip into my skin with each blow. But I have to try.

It's been a long time since he put me in here. I don't know exactly how long, but I'd guess hours. The first time he slowed to a stop, I thought he would get out and try to stop me and shut me up. But he didn't.

He either doesn't care, or he's confident that my struggling and muffled screams are useless. The soft sounds of the car rumbling and moving effortlessly against the smooth asphalt make my eyes shut. My fate's no longer mine, but I still have fight in me. I can't give up hope. I heard my phone go off in the front of the car a while ago. It rang a few times, but there's been nothing since.

I don't know who it was, or if anyone else has called wondering where I am. Maybe he's just shut it off. For all I know, he threw it out the window.

My eyes feel puffy and swollen with tears. I hate this. I hate how helpless I am. I'm bounced around painfully as the car passes over an uneven patch of gravel and then slows. My heart hammers against my chest, and the heavy weight of sleep vanishes, replaced with intense anxiety. We've stopped.

I keep perfectly still as he opens and closes his door. I wait to hear where he's going. Part of me hopes he'll forget I'm back here, like that's even a possibility. Still, if that were the case, I could try to get the fuck out of here.

That stupid dream crumbles into dust as he opens the trunk. I bite down on the gag in my mouth and shake my head, trying to move away from him.

He looks at me with an intense stare that makes me want to cave to him. Something in his look sparks an electric current between us, but in a flash it's gone.

I don't fear him, not like the others. Some part of me feels safe with him. It's a false sense of security, but it's there, keeping me somewhat calm although anger is coursing through me.

He grabs my waist, hoisting me over his shoulder. I try to struggle, but his large hand smacks hard against my ass. *Slap!* His hand meets my bare skin underneath my skirt, and the shocking pain shoots through my body. My back bows, and a scream rips through my throat, muffled by the gag.

"Stop it." His harsh admonishment makes my body go limp. I struggle to take a breath as I look around. There's nothing but woods. I can't see anything but woods.

He's going to kill me. My heart hammers frantically and I nearly vomit, but then I see pavers.

Gorgeous stained concrete pavers make a perfect path surrounding a garden of lavender and rose bushes. Lush green grass trimmed to the perfect height separates the tiles. As we walk up some steps, I see columns with ivy growing up the side and over the roof of a pavilion.

I don't have a chance to see anything else, but we're at a house at least. I know that much. A home with a perfectly manicured, and well taken care of lawn. Which means other people will be here. Hope ignites within me.

I may be in the middle of the woods. But if someone comes, I can yell for help. If I find a way out, I can hide in the trees. The fight in me strengthens as he carries me through the doorway and shuts it behind us with a loud bang.

I look up and see the massive French doors that we walked through. They have a colonial touch to them, all classic lines and stark white coloring. The hardwood floors are dark, with wide planks. If this were any other day, I'd admire the architecture. But this isn't any other day. And this isn't a place to admire, it's a place that induces fear. It's beautiful, but it's still a prison.

Before I have a chance to look around and take in more of my surroundings looking for exits or anything I can use as a weapon, Kade carries me up the stairs and through a dark hallway. A room. He's taking me to a room. My heartbeat picks up.

I can't freak out. I need to pay attention and keep track of where the exit is. We walk much longer than I thought possible. If my count is correct, we pass six doors and an open hallway with a balcony that overlooks the entrance. It's hard to tell how many doors we pass exactly since the hallway is so dark, but when we get to the balcony I'm able to use the lighting to my advantage as I look around.

This house is huge. No, not a house. A mansion, maybe?

All too soon the balcony ends, and once again darkness takes over. I can barely make out a door to my left, and then he stops.

He lowers me to the ground more gently than I thought he would. The zip ties dig deeper into my ankles because of the angle, and I hiss in a breath. I hear keys jingling, and I look up to see an old set of keys in his hands. The keys look like they're made from cast iron, and I'm guessing he pulled them down from a nearby hook on the wall. I hadn't noticed earlier due to the distracting and excruciating pain in my ankles, but I can't make that mistake again. I need to stay alert if I'm going to get out of here alive. Kade carefully selects one key from the bunch although they all look alike to me. With a clink, the door unlocks and he pushes it open.

He looks down at me for a moment, but I'm too scared to look up.

I feel his eyes on me, but I keep my own trained on the ground.

I let out a yelp of surprise as he quickly picks up my small body and takes me into the room, cradling me in his arms. I resist the urge to rest my head against his hard, muscular chest.

My stomach hurts, and the exhaustion hits me harder than before.

He leaves the door open and carries me across the room onto a soft bed before setting me down gently.

He leaves me there, bound, gagged, and lying on my side. I close my eyes, listening to him moving through the room. It's dark, but I can clearly make out a dresser in front of me. It's an antique with glass knobs. I imagine the pulls have screws on the ends. I've seen them before at the hardware store. If I get a chance, I could unscrew them. I could use one to stab him in his jugular and get the fuck out of here. I just need him to untie me first.

I hear him gather items throughout the room and take them out to the hallway.

It seems like forever, listening to him rearranging the room. And then nothing.

It sounds like he's gone. But he's left me bound. I try to look around, but I can't see anything besides the dresser. I wish I could move, but with my hands bound behind my back, I can't. I try again uselessly to get out of the binds, but it only makes the pain worse.

I still as I hear his footsteps in the hallway. They grow closer and louder until he's standing in front of me, his hips by my head. I can see the buckle of his belt, and his crisp white shirt that now has a smear of blood, no doubt from when he carried me.

He grips my forearm and with a quick slice, cuts the ties. Relief flows through me, along with new aches and the need to move. But I'm stiff, waiting for him to cut the ties on my ankles. As soon as he does, I fucking bolt.

I jump up and push against him with all my weight, and by some miracle, it forces him far enough away that I'm able to jump from the bed. I sprint as hard as I can, but I don't make it more than a few feet before his hand grips the hem of my sweater. I let out a shriek, landing hard on my side, palms slamming against the floor as he drags me toward him. All the while I fight. I kick my legs blindly and scream for help.

My foot lands hard against his chest, but he doesn't even flinch. Instead he grips my hair at the base of my skull, and I yelp in agony as he yanks my head back. Tears leak from my eyes at the sharp pain, and my hands instinctively move to try and pry his fingers from my head. He releases my head, but the momentary relief I feel is quickly eclipsed by intense pain once more as he grabs both of my wrists. The stinging pain from the cuts intensifies.

With my wrists secured in one hand, he wraps his other arm around my waist and carries me back to the bed.

He pushes me face down on the bed, his large frame pinning me beneath him, forcing me still. He seizes the nape of my neck and squeezes until I go limp beneath him, surrendering the fight I so badly lost. Tears roll down my cheeks, every part of my body aching, and my soul crushed with hopelessness.

"This is your one warning." His hot breath leaves chills down my spine, his lips barely touching the shell of my ear. A shiver runs through my body and the deep cadence of his voice makes my pussy clench with sinful thoughts. "There is no escape from this."

CHAPTER 4

Olivia

I CAN'T SLEEP FOR MORE THAN A FEW MINUTES at a time. I just can't. I'm afraid to move, afraid to even breathe too loudly. But I have to. I have to look and see if there's a way out.

He has my phone. I hope he still has it. I know I heard the ringtone earlier, so I can only hope Cheryl or someone tracks it and finds me here.

But how long would that take? Too fucking long.

I can't wait for a knight in shining armor to come and save me. Every second I'm here is another second Kade could decide to just kill me, or worse. I shudder as I think back to Ricky and Vic. Some things are definitely worse than death. The first thing I need to do is move. I haven't budged an inch since he left me.

I'm terrified that the moment I move off the bed, he'll burst through the door and beat me. I remember his weight on top of me, and the way he gripped my hair. I can't fight him. It's an uneven match.

He's not going to save me. It was stupid for me to even hope he would. No one's coming to my rescue.

I have to try to save myself.

Without realizing it, I've gathered handfuls of the down comforter. It's fluffy and soft, but the intricate stitching chafes against the cuts on my wrists. With a small sigh I let the comforter fall and gently run a fingertip along my wounds.

I can't stay here and wait for more.

I slowly pull the blanket away from me. I'm still fully clothed in my sweater and skirt. There's no way I'm taking anything off of me. I need as much between me and that asshole as possible.

I gently climb off the bed and head over to the one thing I've been thinking about all night. The windows.

There are two large windows on either side of the large

bed. They're both covered by curtains that run from the floor to the ceiling. The fabric is thick and rich, although with such little light in the room, I can't tell for certain what color the curtains are. I place one foot on the cold hardwood floors and pause before placing my full weight down slowly.

The floors creak, and I wince. My eyes dart to the door and I hold my breath, waiting for a sign that he's heard. It's been hours since he left me alone here, I think. He must be sleeping by now.

We're high up on the second story. I'm sure he's certain I can't escape. I fucking hope he's that confident.

I take another step, trying my best to keep the creaking to a minimum and walk with slow, deliberate steps to the nearest window.

My heart beats loudly in my ears. It climbs up my throat, threatening to suffocate me. What if he finds me trying to escape? What will he do to me?

I shake my head slightly and walk quicker to the window. I can't think like that. I can't let fear keep me from saving myself. I pull back the heavy curtain and nearly cry at what I find. My shoulders sink inward. There are bars on the windows. Thick steel bars. They're on the outside, so I could open a window, but then I'd have to try to squeeze myself through. I don't even think my head would fit, let alone my wider parts.

I swallow, and my dry throat aches from the wretched screaming that did nothing for me. I can't give up. I imagine he locked the door, but I haven't checked. I take two steps toward it, but then I stop as I spot the dresser, remembering the thought I had earlier. The knobs. I need a weapon; I need more than one.

I brace one hand and hover over the knob. I see his tall frame; I feel his lips on my neck. I shouldn't think twice about hurting him. He *deserves* it. He can't do this to me! But I do. I question if I should. I question if I really want to.

The thoughts are gone just as quickly as they came, and I hold on to the anger of being taken and the fear of being trapped.

I quickly try to unscrew a knob, but the first one I try is on so fucking tight. I grip it harder and twist it to the point that it hurts my hand, but it doesn't give at all. I breathe frantically and try the other one on the top drawer. But it doesn't budge either.

I crouch lower to try the next, and hope lights within me as it loosens. I unscrew it, but instead of the glass pull being attached to the screw, the screw itself is still in the drawer. I try opening the drawer as silently as I can, but the thing is old. There aren't any tracks, and it's loud as hell trying to pull it out.

I get it open just enough for my hand to fit inside. The

drawer itself is empty, which I find odd, but I don't give it much thought.

I try to get the screw loose, pushing my thumb against it and twisting, and when that doesn't work, I try using my nails. But it won't fucking move.

Useless.

I lick my lips and drop the knob into the drawer, not bothering to close it as I take a look around the room.

I need to find something else.

The room is massive. Compared to the dorms and my cramped apartment, it's ridiculous in size.

I search the room for closets, but there are none. There are two wardrobes that look identical to the left of the room, however.

As I walk toward them to see what's inside, I nearly trip. A rug I hadn't noticed before is under my feet. I must have fallen onto it earlier, but I hadn't noticed. I steady myself and stare at the door, hoping he didn't hear. Minutes pass with no sign of him.

I walk as quietly as I can to the wardrobes, and pray there's something in there I can use against him.

It doesn't take long for me to get there and find the first one empty. Hope dwindles inside of me, but I have to try the other. With shaky hands, I open the second wardrobe and I find the same. Empty. The feeling of defeat washes over me.

That leaves only one other thing to try, and I shouldn't even be getting my hopes up.

I look to the door to the room, and pray it's unlocked. What are the odds he would be so foolish?

And if it isn't locked, maybe he's waiting for me. Maybe it's a test.

Either way, I have to try. I won't stay here and make this easy on him. I can't. I need to get the fuck out of here. That's the only truth I need to hold on to.

CHAPTER 5

Kade

THE ICE CLINKS IN MY GLASS AS I LIFT IT OFF the coffee table. The fire across the room roars and crackles. Those are the only noises in the room, but the noises I'm hearing are different. I can't stop hearing James' last words. The bang of my gun. Over and over, the sounds won't stop.

Criminal. It was our code word. I keep hearing him say it. We chose that word together, but I'd hoped neither of us would ever have to say it.

"You really going to make me say it again?" My heart twists in my chest as I hear James' words over and over in my mind. I knew this was a possibility when we signed up for this. We both did. It was only supposed to be months, but it turned into years. But if either of us ever had to say that word, I was hoping it'd be me. Not James.

My official record lists thirty-eight confirmed kills overseas. And he had twenty-six. We were something else, so fucking good the government came to us with an opportunity we couldn't pass up. One last job, and we'd earn enough cash we could live off it forever.

We were ready to go in, excited even. It sucked having to go in separate, but it made sense.

Fucking Ricky Stone was harder to crack than they said he'd be. He's a hotheaded fuck, but he still hasn't shown his cards.

Two years ago, one of the biggest sex trafficking trades went down, but neither of us found out about it until it had passed even though we were supposed to be in on it. We—I can't seem to get close enough.

I front the money for the cartel, I'm their largest investor. My fake background has me passing myself off as an ex-con. As far as they know, I served time for money laundering, and the connections I made in prison led to my current interest in dealing in women. That's how the cartel found me, actually. Buying women. Of course the women all went free and are now safe and recovering. But they think I killed them when I was done.

That's what the cartel does. It's what's expected.

Ricky and Vic are sick fucks; they're behind the biggest and most profitable sex slave and drug trafficking rings across the globe. From the United States, to Thailand, and plenty of places in between.

I was so close to getting more information about Ricky's informants and business partners overseas. Or at least the locations where they store the women.

I wonder what James found out. I wonder what he did that tipped them off. Tears prick my eyes and I slam the glass down. Fuck!

And *she* saw. Olivia. She saw me kill him. It's against protocol to do anything illegal when you're undercover. Every action has to be approved first, which is bullshit, and everyone knows it. Even though James told me to kill him, they can't find out. If she went to the police and told them, they'd pull me out in a heartbeat. If she got out and told, this entire operation would be a wash. Years of hard work would be gone, just like that. I could live with that. But my best friend's death would be for nothing. I can't let that happen to James.

I would have killed him for nothing.

For a split second, I considered turning the gun on Ricky, at that cold-blooded, hotheaded prick. I considered just killing him and dying alongside James. It would have been an honorable death.

But the rest of them would have lived, including Vic. And the girls would still have been shipped off. Ricky dying, and maybe one of his henchmen—it wouldn't have been enough to take them down.

And James said it. He said the one word that meant I needed to pull the trigger.

Criminal.

I swallow the whiskey straight from the bottle this time. My head hurts and my throat burns, but my heart hurts more. I'm in too deep to turn back now.

I need to end this, and the date for the sale is quickly approaching. I know it is.

For him, I'll make sure they all die. I'll make sure they pay.

I hear the floor creak above the study. She got out of bed. I grind my teeth, hating the position I'm in.

When I saw her, I thought for a moment I'd done it. I thought I'd pointed the gun at the real enemy, that I'd died. She looked like an angel with her white sweater and sun-kissed skin. Her eyes pleaded with me to save her. They were taking her from me. My angel.

I look down into my empty glass.

There's no angel out there for me.

If I'd left her there with them, I know what they would

have done. I know they would have beaten her and used her body. They would have passed her around before selling her off.

They would have broken her, just like they've done with so many others. I couldn't let it happen, but now I've fucked myself.

I've been trained on what to expect. I know what I need to do so they'll believe me and let me in closer.

I have to break her myself.

CHAPTER 6

Olivia

I HEAR HIM COMING DOWN THE HALL, AND MY head whips to the door. Fuck! I bolt to the bed. I don't have a damn thing to arm myself with.

I get under the covers and lie there. But then I remember the knob. Motherfucking fucker! I want to scream. I ball my hands into fists under the covers and squeeze my eyes shut as the door creaks open.

Why am I so fucking stupid?

I stay as still as possible as he moves closer to the bed. I hear his footsteps as he approaches and my stomach sinks. At the same time though my pussy clenches at the threat of him taking his anger out on me. My cheeks flame. I don't know what's wrong with me that I could want something so demeaning.

The bed dips with his heavy weight and my body rolls slightly, even though I'm stiff.

I bite down hard on my lip.

My mind runs away with the most sexual images. I don't want this. But some sick part of me does.

A sob rips up my throat, and I wish it hadn't. His hand lands softly on my hip, and I just barely resist the urge to take a swing at him and push him away from me. I could try to run again. I *should* try to run again. But at the same time, the thought of him pinning me down makes me equally turned on and fearful.

"I should punish you." His calm, deep voice stops my thoughts where they were.

I shudder and curl slightly away from him.

"Do you think what you've done wasn't defying me?" he asks in an even voice.

His weight shifts and he lifts off the bed. I don't turn to see what he's doing, but my eyes pop open wide and my breathing pauses as I realize what he's noticed. I hear him snort and push the dresser drawer in.

Fuck. Fuck. He walks over to the window and moves the curtains.

I left a fucking trail for him. I feel him behind me and I want to cower, but I remain still.

"I asked you a question." His voice is soft, as though there's no threat. But I know there is.

I take a ragged breath. "Yes."

"Yes, you thought you weren't defying me?" he asks with a lowered tone, daring me to confirm what he's said. I hesitate to answer. I don't know what to say.

In a flash he rips the sheets from me and I cower from him. My body trembles as he grips my hips and brings me closer to him. My pussy heats, and I can't stand it. I hate how my body is betraying me. I shouldn't be so turned on by him, but I can't help the effect he's having on me.

"Please!" I cry out as I resist the urge to fight him.

He whispers in my ear, "What did you think would happen, Olivia?"

I shake my head. I don't know what to say, so I say nothing, and it angers him.

"Answer me!" he yells as his hand comes down hard on my ass. He pushes me down on the mattress, his large hand splayed against my shoulder blades, pinning me down. I struggle against him, trying to get away.

"You're only making it worse on yourself." His words register and I try to stay still.

"Please don't." I swallow my pride as I beg him. I may be turned on. I may find him handsome, and a sick part of me thinks this could fulfill a fantasy I've never shared with anyone before. But I don't want this.

"What did you think would happen when you defied me?" he asks.

"I didn't." I respond with the truth as a small sob escapes my lips. "I didn't think."

"You should've, angel." He lowers his head to mine and gently kisses my hair. His pet name for me seems off, but comforting somehow. "With everything you do, there will be consequences. Good and bad."

He moves back as his hand leaves my ass. His fingers gently walk up my thigh, pulling my skirt up and exposing me.

"Please don't," I beg him again. I can't help that the shivers that run up my spine harden my nipples and make my clit throb with need. The threat of him using me leaves me breathless with both desire and fear. I don't know which outweighs the other. But I won't give in. This is wrong.

"There are consequences," he says confidently. "I told you that."

Smack! His hand comes down hard again as he spanks my ass and the pain rips through me. I scream and take the blow. And then another. The weight of his body holds me down.

"What were you going to do with whatever you were looking for?" he asks. It's a trick question. I know it is.

I shake my head and part my lips to answer, but instead a shriek comes out as his hand whips my ass again.

"Do not lie to me." His words are hard.

"Defend myself!" I manage to bite out. That's the truth and if he doesn't like it, then I guess he can just beat me. Fighting against him is the same thing as defending myself. So long as I'm here, I'll fight.

"Oh sweetheart," he whispers as his lips graze my neck. My body betrays me yet again, and I hate the wave of arousal rolling through me as he plants a sweet kiss on my neck.

"There's no fighting this." He pulls my body toward the edge of the bed, holding me under him. "There's no way out."

"Please," I say, but I'm not sure what I'm pleading for as his hands lift my skirt up.

"Do you know who I am, angel?" he asks as his thumb rips through my cotton panties. Kade tears the thin pair as though they're nothing, exposing me to him.

I shake my head into the pillow, denying everything. This isn't real. This isn't happening. He takes the opportunity to answer his own question.

"I'm a bad man. And now you *belong* to me." His words shatter any hope I had. My throat closes as fear threatens to overwhelm me.

"This," he says as his hand cups my pussy, "this belongs to me."

As he says the words, I smell whiskey on his breath, but it only adds to my arousal for him. Goddamn traitor body.

He pulls back quickly with shock, and then pushes his fingers against my heated core.

"You're fucking soaked. You *want* this." Shame washes through me again. It's one thing to be turned on, but it's another thing entirely for him to know. It's my treacherous body. My own depraved fantasies. But this is reality.

I shake my head. "I don't." I barely push the words out.

He pulls his hand away and yanks my sweater over my head. I try to fight against him, but it's useless. I cross my arms over my chest feeling so demeaned and helpless. My tank top and bra are the only things keeping me from being completely bared to him.

"You will remove them." His voice hardens as he adds, "Or I will." He stares at me, waiting for me to comply. I don't want him to. But I don't want to do it either.

Slowly I pull the tank top away and unhook my bra, letting it fall. I can't look at him.

He balls all of my clothes in his hands and moves off the bed. Leaving me there naked, embarrassed and completely fucking soaked for him.

I wait for him to do something—anything. But he just watches me.

"Do you know about BDSM or anything at all about Master slave relationships?" he asks.

My blood boils. I know all about them. I've read about them in books, but this shit is real life. "Yes." I push the word out through my teeth.

"Do you know what you are to me now?" he asks.

I barely shake my head as his eyes pierce into me.

"All you are is mine. All you will do is what I say. I am your *Master* now. There is no safe word, there is only you obeying what I tell you to do."

I bite my tongue and resist the urge to snap at him.

"I will always keep you safe. I will never do anything to hurt you. I won't push you beyond what's needed. I promise you that." I don't believe a word he says.

"You'll behave now, or things will only get worse for you," he says in a voice laced with sympathy. He's not sorry though. He did this to me. He chose to do this. He *wants* to do this.

I swallow thickly, hating that every part of me is begging to make him happy. I can't avoid the inevitable, but maybe I can prolong it, if I behave.

"You need to be good for me," he says with a low voice. "You're going to learn how to be the perfect slave, pet, fucktoy. Whatever it is that's required from you." My breath halts in my lungs, and fear freezes my body.

"You're a reflection of me, and you *will* be perfect. Is that understood?"

"Yes," I answer him, feeling completely defeated. The word is choked as it leaves my lips.

"Good girl." His hand gentles on my back. "Tomorrow you'll have another chance. Don't disappoint me."

The seconds pass slowly and finally he leaves the room. As soon as he's gone I cover myself, hiding underneath the duvet.

Anger replaces my shame and fear. I don't care what he does to me, I'll never break for him. Never.

CHAPTER 7

Olivia

I WAKE UP TO THE SOUNDS OF KADE MOVING IN the room. I stay perfectly still under the covers; hopeful he hasn't noticed I'm awake. I can't see him, so I don't know what he's doing. I just want him to leave.

I've barely slept at all. I have no way to get out of here, and no hope of leaving. *Yet*, I tell myself. I just need to get out of this room first. One step at a time.

"I know you're awake." His words ring out clear in the

quiet room. I hear him push a drawer shut and walk closer to the bed.

"I brought in breakfast. Come." He gives the order and it pisses me off.

"No," I say from under the covers, like a petulant child. But I don't care. I'm not going to go to him.

Silence greets me.

"You're disobeying me?" he asks in that low threatening voice that somehow fools my body into thinking I should get wet and hot for him. I bite my bottom lip, ignoring him and my arousal.

"Get up and get on your knees."

I ignore the part of me that's dying to obey him and hold on to the sane part of me. I grit my teeth. I'm not doing that. I fucking refuse to let him use me. I poke my head up beyond the covers and look him in the eyes.

They're the softest shade of blue; they could be cold and callous, or forgiving and sympathetic. He could use them to charm women and convince them to be his. They're eyes filled with deceit. I don't trust him. I'll never trust him.

"Fuck you." I hold his eyes as they narrow and heat with lust. It shocks me to the core. Desire. His eyes flame with desire, and I can't help that his look makes my own needs flare.

"Is that what you want?" he asks in a deep, menacing voice that only manages to turn me on as he unbuckles his belt. The hardness in his features softens, and a small grin forms on his face as he slides the belt from the loops.

"I wasn't going to fuck you just yet. But maybe that's why you're having such a hard time realizing what you are now."

My mouth tries to part with lust, but I slam it shut. The tension between us is thick. But it's wrong, and I hate it. This isn't supposed to be like this.

He loops the belt in his hand. "I said get on your knees." With a flick of his wrist he whips the belt in his hand with a loud *smack!* It makes me flinch and my pussy clench.

I grind my teeth and shake my head. "No."

Smack! The belt falls hard onto my thighs. I scream out and he pulls the covers back.

"Knees!" he yells at me, and I bury my head into the mattress, huddling into a ball.

He grips my hips and pulls me toward him. I scramble to get away, but he holds me there and presses his chest to my back. I try elbowing him and the first time it works, I hit something, but it fucking hurts me more than it seems to hurt him.

He pushes his weight against me and shushes me in my ear. Like I'm a wild animal, and he's trying to calm me.

"Let me tell you a secret, angel." He speaks clearly as I still beneath him. "I don't want to hurt you." Liar. He's a fucking liar.

He continues talking as if he read my mind. "I have no choice but to train you. You may not understand why, and honestly, you don't need to know. But I don't have to hurt you. This doesn't have to be a fight."

His words are soothing, and I almost start to relax a little, but the next thing he says comes out hard. "But you will listen to me. And I've found it's best when punishment is severe."

"Fuck you!" I scream again.

"Don't make me punish you.""Do whatever the fuck you want, asshole." I sneer.

"What I want is to feed you," he says simply. "But you disobeyed me. So you need to be punished first."

"Please stop this." The words come out without my conscious awareness. "You don't have to do this." I sound weak and pathetic as I beg him.

I expect him to laugh. I expect him to tell me he won't stop. Instead he hesitates. For a moment, I feel something. I feel hope.

He moves away from the bed and I look back at him, praying he'll set me free. But there's no mercy in his expression.

"I do," he finally says. He nods his head slowly, keeping my gaze with his intense stare. "I have to do this. And you have to obey me, either by choice or force. That's entirely up to you. But it's going to happen."

My eyes fall. "Just kill me then." Again I speak without thought.

"I can't do that." He speaks so quietly I barely hear him say, "I need you." The way his voice comes out with so much sincerity makes me believe him.

"Now come over here and eat."

I eye him warily. "You said I had to be punished first."

"I did. And I changed my mind." He leans closer to me. "You should move quickly, before I change my mind again."

I look up at him, not knowing what to do. In an instant, my anger dissipates. My throat seems to swell with a lump that won't go down. "I have a mother." I try to speak confidently, but my voice comes out raspy. I look down and try to calm myself.

I back away as he sits next to me and pulls me closer to him. I try to resist, but it's no use. He gently pets my back.

"You have family. You have friends," he says calmly, and it kills the last bit of hope I have, like an ice shard through my heart. "I know you do. I know their names. I know where they live." My eyes pop open and my body chills with fear.

"Don't worry, I don't have any plans to hurt them. I meant it when I said I didn't want to hurt you, either." He tilts my head up to force me to look into his blue eyes. "I mean it. But you *need* to listen."

He stares at me for a long time, waiting until he has my full attention. "You've gotten yourself into the middle of something very serious. There's no way you can get out."

I shake my head, wanting to deny it, wanting to plead with him.

"Hush, angel." He rubs his thumb along my jaw and I subconsciously lean into his touch. "There's no changing that now. The only thing you have control over is how you respond to me."

I stare into his eyes, trying to understand. "They want me to train you. You know that, don't you?"

I barely nod my head as I accept that reality. "I've trained sex slaves before. Some willing, and some not so much." He pushes the hair out of my face. "It's easier when they're willing."

I can't look at him.

"If that's the way you want it, we can do it that way, too." He moves away from me and I scoot closer to the headboard, keeping my eyes on him as prey watches a predator.

"You need to eat," he says simply.

"I'm not hungry," I whisper.

"Do you need to use the bathroom?" he asks.

I shake my head and hug my knees to my chest. My entire body feels hollow. I don't need anything other than a chance to get away from him. As I shake my head, I become acutely aware of the pressure in my bladder. But I'm not having that fucker watch me go to the bathroom. I'll hold it as long as I have to. I'd rather pee in the corner.

He sighs angrily and presses his lips into a straight line. "If you need something, you'll need to knock loudly. Do you understand?" His voice is hard.

I nod my head as I say, "Yes."

He leaves the plate from the tray and walks out of the room without another word. I wait a moment, thinking he's left it unlocked and quietly move to the door. I'm halfway there when I hear the click and see the knob rattle as he tests to make sure it's locked.

My heart falls in my chest.

He's going to train me for them. That's all I am now. And there's no escape.

I suppose one would experience many different emotions when faced with something like this, the first being denial. And maybe that's what I spent the last few hours and yesterday doing. But the second emotion is anger.

I look around the room and let the rage consume me. And then I do something very, very stupid.

CHAPTER 8

Olivia

HE CAN'T JUST TAKE ME AND EXPECT ME TO bend to his whims. He thinks he's my *Master*. He can go fuck himself. I'm not some sort of sweet little thing, so desperate to live I'll let him whittle me down into nothing. I refuse to give in to him. I take out the bottom drawer of the dresser. Or rather, I rip it out. I pick it up by the handle.

It's fucking heavy and made of real wood, but I'm able to swing it with all my weight against the side of the armoire.

It barely breaks, and that makes me even angrier. I scream out and swing it again. This time it cracks and splinters, and falls into large pieces. One board almost lands on my foot, but I move it in time.

I pick up a small splinter that split off and shove it under the duvet in the bed. I'll start storing weapons.

I breathe heavily, staring at the armoire. I want that fucking door. I can see myself smashing it over his head. Or maybe using it as a shield to break down the bedroom door. It looks heavy, but I only need one chance. I toss the board onto the floor and grab the door to the armoire, tugging it, trying to bring it down.

I hold onto the door as the armoire tilts and gravity takes over as it falls to the floor with a loud crash. My hand on the door slips, and it smacks my arm as it falls. Fuck! That hurt like a bitch. It's definitely going to leave a bruise. I almost kick the damn thing in my rage, but that'd be worthless.

Instead I grip it and pull, trying to break it off. I'm tearing this fucking door off, and then I'm smashing through the door to the bedroom keeping me prisoner. I'll fucking break my way out of here.

"What the fuck!" The door slams open and Kade stares back at me with a look of contempt.

"What the fuck are you doing?" he sneers at me. My chest heaves. I don't know. I have no fucking clue what I'm doing, but it doesn't matter. It was my choice. And I'll do whatever I want.

He stalks toward me and I grab a piece of the drawer that broke off. I point the jagged edge at him. He wants to tame me, break me, fuck me... well then he's going to have to fight me first.

"What are you going to do with that, angel?" His dark voice sends a warning that makes my breathing come in frantic pants. I ignore the pulsing desire deep in my core.

I can see him overpowering me, ripping my weapon from my hand and making me pay for disobeying him. But he just punished me last time. Tears prick my eyes and my throat closes as a lump grows. I don't want this. I don't want any of this. This is some fucked up twisted mix of a nightmare and fantasy.

Kade pauses on his way to me, sensing my anger starting to wane. He holds his hand up like he's approaching a wounded animal. And maybe that's what I am. But he made me this way. It's his fault. I fucking hate him.

"Olivia, put it down." No fucking way. I shake my head and hold up the board with my trembling hand. I try to steady it, but I can't.

The reality of the situation hits me like a ton of bricks. I'm fucking dead. I can't fight him. Even with this board, I don't stand a chance. But at least I'm trying.

I shake my head again and the second I blink away the

tears, he's on me. I scream as his body slams against mine and he pushes me down onto the rug. He grabs the board before I can do anything and pulls it from me.

I thrash under him, but his weight is too heavy. He cages me in, leaning his chest against mine.

"Shh, it's alright. Calm down." He whispers comforting words into my ear. His hand rubs along my hip and up my side then back down in soothing strokes. His lips barely touch my neck with his head safely nestled in the crook of my neck. The position also forces me still, unable to move much at all.

Minutes pass. My racing heart starts to slow, and the adrenaline rushing in my blood begins to melt away. I lie still under him, not knowing what he's going to do next.

"You shouldn't have done that, angel," he says after a long while. His hand steadies on my hip.

"I'm sorry." The words slip past my lips instinctively. Am I sorry? No, I'm not sorry. Not right now. I don't know what the consequences will be, but right now, I'm not sorry.

"Did you really think having a tantrum was going to help you at all?" He tsks in my ear.

He slowly rises, pinning my wrists down at my side. It's only then do I feel his raging erection against my hip. My eyes widen, and I force myself to look anywhere but at him.

I can't breathe.

"Get on your knees, angel." I shake my head, but I'm not

given any choice. He flips me over and splays his hand on my shoulders, leaving me prostrate and completely vulnerable to him.

My breathing comes in ragged pants. "This would hurt to spank you with, angel," he says as he places a piece of the broken armoire against my bare ass. I hold my breath waiting for the blow. But nothing comes.

"You've already hurt yourself with your display of disobedience, haven't you?" His fingers gently touch my arm and I wince. I can't see, but I'd be damned if there isn't already a bruise there.

His fingers run along my spine and down to my ass. He leans down and plants a tender kiss on my neck. "I understand, angel. I do. But you can't behave this way." My pussy heats, and my back bows. I instantly regret it, but he doesn't seem to notice. Shame replaces my arousal. He places another sweet kiss on the nape of my neck this time, pushing my hair out of his way.

"I can't allow it," he says with a deep voice laced with regret.

Smack! His hand comes down hard on my ass. *Smack!* The pain shoots through my body. It's a sharp, stinging pain. My skin reddens with his repeated blows until I'm crying hysterically into the rug.

My ass and thighs sting. My eyes are swollen with tears. "Shh," he tries to comfort me, leaning down to kiss me again, but I pull away. I hate him. I hate him with everything in me.

"Now now, angel, you knew this would happen. Didn't you?"

I hate how he makes it seem like it was my fault. How could anyone blame me for trying to get out of here? I don't want this.

"I told you, you need to be good for me." I bite my tongue to keep myself from telling him to fuck off. I don't want any more punishment. He leans down to comfort me again with his hand still on my stinging ass, and again I move away from him.

"Let me comfort you, angel." No, fuck that. He hurt me, I won't seek shelter from him. No matter how much I want it. He pulls me into his arms and although I don't fight back, I don't lean into him either.

My ass burns as he moves me closer to him. I try not to whimper and hold it in. I won't let him see how much it hurts.

"I don't want to hurt you, angel." I hate that he keeps saying that. If he didn't want to hurt me, then he wouldn't. It's as simple as that.

"I wanted to keep you to myself, but now you've given me no choice." My heart rate picks up. "I don't have much time, and it's obvious you're going to fight me."

I risk a glance back at him as he says, "I'm sorry, angel." I don't believe him for one second. I know the sympathy and compassion in his eyes are complete bullshit. "I didn't want this for you." He's a liar.

Tears roll down my cheeks and I don't even bother to brush them away. He lays a hand on my cheek and I hate that it brings me warmth. "Please," I beg him again, "just let me go."

"If only you knew." I turn away from him, hating how he's acting like this is out of his control.

He huffs a humorless laugh. "I'm taking you to a place where you won't get away with this. You'll be running to me to keep you safe."

My body chills at his words.

"I won't let them hurt you." I look deep into his eyes and some naïve part of me believes him.

"But you won't get away with this shit over there."

CHAPTER 9

Kade

I LOCK THE DOORS ON THE CAR AND THINK about checking the trunk. It's been quiet, but I don't trust her being quiet. It's been five hours. I drove straight through the entire time. I'm sure she needs to relieve herself and stretch. But maybe she's quiet because she's asleep. I fucking hope that's it. She's going to need to be well-rested so she can take this in.

I remember the way she struggled in my arms trying to

get her back in the trunk. I'm a sick fuck, but feeling her na- ked body writhing against me made me want to overpower her even more.

I thought about just letting her go. Leaving the door open and letting her leave.

But they'd just give me someone else at this point.

The meet is coming up fast. He needs to trust me, and this is how that'll happen.

I need this to work. There's no turning back.

And they gave me *her*.

I have to will away the image of me punishing her. Fuck, I groan and lean my head back. I still can't believe what I wanted to do to her.

I'm on the edge of unleashing a side of me that I don't want others to see. A depraved part of me I'm scared to un- leash.

When she opens that smart mouth of hers I want so badly to put it to good use.

Last night was a turning point for me, with her acting out and the constant disobedience. On one hand, I under- stand it; I respect it even. On the other, I want to spank her ass raw and then give her what she really needs. What we *both* need.

I didn't used to be a bad man. I'm not sure at what point that changed for me. But seeing her look up at me with heated desire in her eyes and continuing to push me, knowing she was going to be punished begs me to release a beast inside of me that's clawing to get to her.

I stare up at Gabriel's mansion and admire its beauty. The intricately carved columns and flagstone pathways grace his home. It's luxurious outside, and even more lavish inside. But it's a house of pure sin and decadence of every sort. My dick starts hardening as I walk up the steps.

My handler, Gates, keeps saying I'm in too deep. He's threatened to pull me twice. I've never once thought he was right until I started thinking about my relationship with Gabriel Durand, a French entrepreneur who brought his expertise here stateside.

He owns this place, and runs it and the illicit parties that occur inside. He doesn't deal in women, but he keeps them. Not for him, but for others. It's not just a brothel, it's something much more. Dirtier and dark. This mansion is a place of pure sin.

I remember the first time I came here, to see how the women were trained. Men and women bring their own *pets*, or they come and pay for their choice.

Olivia needs to see what's expected of her. This is only going to help her to learn faster. I want to see how she reacts. I want to know what she really thinks of this.

If she's terrified and still fighting, I'm fucked. I won't do it. I can't do this to her. I'll have to find some excuse and get her the fuck out of here. I can at least save her.

But there's a chance she'll react like other women have here. I've seen the way Gabriel handles them. She could do that for me. I hope she enjoys it. I hope it turns her on. If the desire in her eyes is any indication, this will make the transition easy for her. The idea of her willing to be my pet should make me relieved. It would mean this will be easier and I can move forward with my mission.

Instead it makes me hard as fuck. I'm practically leaking in my pants at the thought of her on her knees and at my mercy.

I close my eyes and will the images away.

This is a mission. I need to stay focused. This isn't about any twisted fantasy I have. This isn't about either one of us.

I'll be quick and make the necessary arrangements so I can begin her training as soon as possible.

I walk quickly up the steps and bang on the hard, maple doors with the cast iron knocker. There's a doorbell, but I never use it. I prefer the feel of the knocker. The raw metal and hard bang remind me of that first night that I spent here when I was doing my research.

The door opens and a short woman with smooth, milky skin answers. Her long, straight blonde hair is pulled into a tight ponytail. Her clear blue eyes shine out with happiness once she registers me.

Her soft voice is just barely audible as she bows her head slightly and moves to the side for me to enter as she respectfully greets, "Good to see you, Master K." I gently set my hand down on her shoulder and step inside.

"You look lovely, Talia." She's in a floor-length silk charmeuse navy dress. It's loose on her. And no doubt will be taken off once evening approaches and the nighttime festivities start.

Talia is different from the others; she belongs to Gabriel. *She* is his most prized possession.

"Is your Master home, Talia?" I ask as she closes the door.

"Yes, Master K," she answers obediently. She raises her head and gestures gracefully with her hand to the right. "May I?" she asks.

The foyer is large with textured walls the color of soft cream, and sconces that give an Old World feel. The curved stairway has a cast iron railing that contrasts with the pale gray and white marbled floors. In the very center is an ancient table, and above it hangs a large crystal chandelier.

Decadence at its finest.

"Lead the way."

Talia's been with Gabriel for nearly a decade now. She didn't come here willingly like the other women. I often watch her and Gabriel. She is his *esclave*, French for slave. At first I was pissed to hear him call her a slave constantly. It took me a long time to realize it, but to the two of them means something else, something more.Our steps echo off the floors. It seems empty, but I know there are others here. This place is never empty, and at night it truly comes alive.

"Are you well?" I ask her as she leads me to a room I've been in before many times. Gabriel's office is just as spacious as every other room in his home. It smells of wood oil and cigars. The room appears dark due to the rich mahogany furniture and deep red handwoven rug that covers most of the floor. But the thick curtains in front of the windows are also drawn, heightening the effect.

A faint blushes rises to her cheeks. "I am. And you?" she asks.

"You've brought me an unexpected guest, *esclave*." Gabriel stands from behind his desk and smiles wide at me.

Talia waits patiently by the door with her head bowed, and her hands clasped as he walks over to me.

Gabriel's a tall man. He's not muscular, but toned—it means he's not an obvious threat, but he's still lethal. He's ruthless in business. And he makes everything his business. I came here first when I went undercover. I had to become part of the scene, and that meant being talked about.

Talking is what Gabriel does best.

His dark hair is slicked back, and his brilliant smile is just as white as his crisp button-down shirt.

He gives me a quick hug along with a hard pat on the back. "I've been waiting for you to show your face in here again."

I never know how he's able to suck me in. No one knows me anymore; I don't even know who I am. But Gabriel does. He has a way of putting me at ease. It's a false sense of security, but it feels... thrilling.

A darkness I've tried to suppress creeps up on me. I need to contain the person I am when I'm here. For Olivia.

He lets a short, throaty laugh out from his chest and looks back at his desk.

"Have a seat, my friend." At first when I met him, I assumed he called all of his guests his friends. I found out very quickly he doesn't.

"Talia, come." He takes a seat and waits as Talia lowers herself beside his desk and sits her knees down on a pillow. He puts a hand on her shoulder and rubs soothing circles over her bare skin.

Her eyes close and she relaxes under his touch.

"I have a problem, Gabriel." I look at Talia as I use Gabriel's first name. It's a rule in his mansion that first names aren't used around pets or slaves. He once told me that for training purposes it's important they only ever know you as Master. But his favorite pet knows him by all his names. And he seems to give her more and more exceptions every time I see them.

"And does that problem have a woman's name?" he asks with a humorous glint in his eye.

"She does. Olivia Bell." Saying her name makes my heart

still in my chest. A part of me wants to keep her a secret. To make sure she's safe. But she's not. I can't keep her safe. "I wasn't prepared for her. And she's quite…"

"Difficult?" he asks with a smirk. "The best ones always are." He looks down at Talia and she must feel his eyes on him, because she looks up. She gives him a small smile and rests her cheek on his thigh.

"I need a room, if you have one available."

"For you? Of course," he replies. Gabriel's always willing to lend a hand. But I'm sure he keeps a record of everyone who's ever owed him anything. I try to lean back in my seat, but I'm too anxious.

"Thank you. I appreciate it." I imagine this is going to cost at least 200 grand. Maybe more, depending on how long she takes.

"You're just in time, too," Gabriel says. I raise my brows in question. "I'm having a celebration tonight."

He reaches down and cups Talia's chin, giving her a small, chaste kiss before looking back at me.

"You've never brought your own before. This should be fun."

CHAPTER 10

Olivia

I SLOWLY WAKE, FEELING GROGGIER THAN I DID when I passed out in the trunk. And hot. So fucking hot. I try to sit up, but then I realize I'm on the floor. My eyes pop open and adrenaline shoots through me. Memories of yesterday come flooding back. Fuck, no. No. I close my eyes and wish it was a dream. But it's not. This is real. Was it yesterday? Or two days ago? How long has it been?

I see movement to my left, and I instinctively jump back.

"Now, angel, that's no way to greet me." His eyes hold a threat I haven't seen before.

"Get on your knees."

His words haunt me. Scenes from yesterday flash before my eyes. I lower myself to my knees slowly and wait. Outside the bedroom I can hear noises. Other people, although I can't make out what they're doing. At first I get the inclination to scream for help. But then I realize he brought me here for a reason. Whoever's outside that door is on his side, not mine.

"You can listen to me," he says with feigned amusement. Fucking prick.

He holds out a glass of water in front of me. But I'm not a fucking idiot. I'm not drinking that, or eating anything he gives me. I don't know what he might have put in it. "Drink," he commands with a deep voice that makes me question my resolve.

I take the glass in my hand and hold it, but I can't bring it to my lips.

He takes the glass from my hands and waits for me to look at him. When I do, he keeps my gaze and takes a sip before handing it back to me. My cheeks burn. I hate that he can read me. Not that anyone in my position wouldn't be easy to read. I'm an emotional wreck.

"Olivia, I'm trying very hard to make this easy for you. You need to obey me."

My blood boils with his bullshit. *Make this easy on me.* My bottom lip trembles, but not from sadness, from anger.

I bring the glass to my lips, but I still don't drink. I can't look at him. I can't look at the glass. I let it fall, and it drops to the ground. The glass doesn't break, but it spills the water on the floor, splashing my leg.

He grabs the nape of my neck with a bruising force, lifting me to my feet so that my head is closer to him. So close, his lips barely touch my cheek. I can feel the heat of his hard body pressing down on top of me. He leans forward, growling in my ear. "Why do you always defy me?"

His hard, chiseled body presses against me. I close my eyes as I feel his erection dig into my stomach. A warmth flows through me as my nipples harden. "You will listen to me."

"Yes, Kade." The words stumble from my mouth.

"Master," he whispers in my ear with a deep, rough voice. "Master K." His grip loosens.

"Yes, Master K." I swallow thickly, waiting for him to release me.

"You're going to learn quickly to obey me. I want you to be perfect. And tonight, you'll see what that means."

Kade reaches into his pocket, and before I can see what he has, he snaps it around my neck. It's not tight and hangs just above my collarbone, but it feels as though it's strangling me.

My heart clenches with betrayal. I don't know why I keep waiting for him to let me go, but I do. I keep hoping he'll see how wrong this is.

"You will obey me," he says sternly, but I don't look at him. I don't respond at all.

"Angel, don't make me angry." He crouches down so he's level with me, and I'm forced to look into his cold blue eyes. But I'm surprised to see they're not cold at all. They're heated, and he stares at me as though he's holding back something dangerous.

It steals my breath from me.

"I'm trying very hard to go easy on you. I want to make this transition as easy as possible. But if I need to remind you of your punishment earlier, I will."

He holds my eyes for a moment, but then backs away. He leaves me on the floor, grabbing a thin piece of fabric from the dresser behind me.

"I want you to wear this tonight." His voice is soft and sincere.

He picks the garment up so I can see. It's a somewhat sheer shift dress with thin silver straps that cross in the back. The straps also look like they would wrap around my throat like a necklace. The dress is a pale blush color—so pale, it's almost white.

He raises his brows and waits. Clothing. Yes, I want that. I'm quick to lift my arms, although that means my breasts are just hanging there for him to see. His eyes travel along my body with appreciation. My pussy clenches despite myself, and I bite down on my lip. I look away as he slips the dress over my shoulders. I just need to cover myself with something.

The soft fabric feels lavish against my skin, although my ass is still raw from yesterday.

He circles me and pulls my hair out from under the dress. His hands linger on my skin and make my eyes close from the comforting touch.

He sighs and sounds disappointed. "Next time I'll be more prepared." I'm not sure if he's talking to me or to himself.

"You still look beautiful, but next time I'll make sure you're ready for them." His eyes linger on my breasts and I realize my nipples are hard.

"Are you cold?" he asks with a smirk. *Asshole.*

I don't respond, and have to seriously resist showing my anger.

He leans his head down and whispers against my neck. "You look utterly fuckable, Olivia. Especially when you tempt me like that." His hand fists the hair at the nape of my neck. He pulls slightly, just to the point of pain and exposes my neck to him.

He plants gentle kisses behind my ear and down my neck. "You make me want to do bad things when you disrespect me like that."

He pulls back and stares at my lips. They're parted, and I swear he's going to kiss me. But he doesn't. He pulls away from me and walks to the dresser. I watch him as he adds cufflinks to complete his ensemble.

"Would you like that, angel?" he asks.

"Would I like what?" I ask him warily.

"If I did bad things to you?"

My eyes linger on his broad shoulders and then down his muscular frame. The faint smell of his scent lingers, a mix of woodsy pine and cigars. I would. Some fucked up part of me wants him to do very bad things to me. But those aren't the words that come out.

"No," I answer with bated breath, and he pauses his movements, looking at me expectantly. "Master K." He gives me a small, approving smile.

"Good girl." He looks in the mirror and then back at me with a devilish glint in his eyes. "I wish you wouldn't lie to me though."

My cheeks heat and I look away to avoid his gaze. It's the first time I really take in the room.

It's luxurious, and by far the most beautiful room I've ever stepped foot in. All the furniture is modern and dark with clean lines. But the linens are a soft white with silver threading. The overall feel is bright and airy, with a fresh atmosphere. It's a con though. I may as well be in a fucking dungeon.

I hear noises outside the room, and for a moment I think it's someone coming in here. I shuffle closer to Kade and grip onto his leg, staring at the door, but the noises pass and no one comes in.

He looks down where my hands are and then to my face. I'm quick to take a step back and flash him a hateful look.

He doesn't like that, and I wish I could take it back. My cheeks heat and I look down, hating that his approval is something I need for survival.

"This is your home for the time being. I'll make sure you have everything you need." I nod my head once, although I don't really consider what he's saying. Anxiety is still racing through my blood.

"We're going downstairs. You will not say a word. Do you understand?" I don't know what it is, his anger, maybe his dominance, but something about the threat in his voice makes me want him even more. It shouldn't, but it does.

"Yes, Kade," I answer. His eyes narrow, and my heartbeat picks up with fear. I don't know why he's upset.

"Master K," he corrects me.

"Master K," I repeat as quickly as I can, and he relaxes his shoulders.

"When we're here you can call me Kade, so long as we're alone. But down there, you will call me Master K."

I nod my head, keeping my eyes on him. He said not

to speak, so I won't. Even though I feel like I should. It's confusing.

Something shifts inside of me. I don't mind his anger so much when I know what I've done to cause it. I expect it. I can't help that I want to fight him. And he should fucking expect it. But the fact he got angry and I didn't know why... I don't like that. Not at all. I don't want it to happen again. At least when I'm pushing him I feel like I have some control. I need that. I need to know what to expect from him, and that's dependent on what I do.

I look up at him and realize I've taken a step closer. My hands are outstretched, ready to touch him.

"It's alright, angel." Kade pets my hair as I try to back away from him. I hate myself for doing that. I don't know why I keep thinking he's the one who's going to save me. He's the reason I'm here.

"Hands out," he says gently, and I slowly will my arms to obey. In an instant both of my wrists are bound in thin silver shackles that are more like bracelets from Pandora than handcuffs, but they're attached by a loop and he's quick to set a lock to bring them together. The snap of the lock makes my pussy clench. This is so wrong.

I stare down at my wrists not wanting to accept it, but somehow I have.

Kade attaches a leash around the loop on the bracelets and leads me from the room.

"I want you to walk beside me." Kade speaks to me as though I have a choice. My body seems to move of its own accord.

"I'm going to show you something tonight, angel. I'm going to show you lots of things, in fact." He brushes the hair out of my face and cups my chin.

"I want you to try to enjoy this. If you don't, this is going to be much harder for you than it has to be."

CHAPTER 11

Olivia

KADE OPENS THE DOOR, AND A FLOOD OF SOUNDS pours into the room. At first all I hear are the sounds of laughter and chatter. The faint sounds of music and people moving about, like this is all normal. If I didn't know any better, I'd think I was hearing just a normal party. I search his face for any sort of indication that this is dangerous.

If he was nervous I'd think I could maybe escape. There'd be some hope left. That I could somehow get away.

He's nothing but confident. He turns to face me and looks me in the eyes. "Behave, angel."

A flood of arousal pulls between my legs, and my chest reddens with a flush of excitement. I try to ignore it, but I'm painfully aware of the effect he has on me.

It's the tenor in his voice, the way he commands me and my body. It's wrong. But it tempts me to give in to him.

I look out across the hall and it almost seems like we're in a hotel. There's a row of numbered doors across the way.

One door is open, and inside a woman is on a swing. It'd odd and made up of steel bars, almost like a chair. Her legs are spread wide and strapped to each end of the legs of the chair. As I realize her wrists are bound to the ropes of the swing, a man steps into view stroking his dick and circling her.

Chills run down my body.

I take a step back and want to fucking run.

I'm not going out there. I pull away, and the chains on the leash clink together. Kade looks back at me with a scowl.

"I need one thing," he growls as he slams the door shut behind him. I try to take a step back, my heart racing in my chest. I've never seen him like this. He's angry as he approaches me.

He takes a step toward me and I take a step back, with my hands bound in front of me and the leash attached.

Kade stops in his tracks and takes a moment to breathe.

The hard lines of his face soften, and he inhales deeply before letting out a long exhale. "Olivia." Hearing my name on his lips loosens the fear in me.

He starts to say something, but I interrupt him.

"I'm scared." I shake my head and swallow thickly. "Please," I say. The fear is more real now than it's ever been. When I'm alone with Kade, this situation doesn't seem real. Maybe it's my attraction to him. Or something about him taking me from those other men. I don't know what it is, but it's different.

But seeing the other man and knowing there are more here? I don't want that. I'm terrified.

Kade takes a step forward with his hand out to cup my chin, his fingers are gentle on my neck. "It's going to be a bit of a shock, angel." I stiffen under his touch. No! I don't want to go down there. His other hand grips the back of my neck and he leans forward, his lips nearly touching mine. His low voice responds to my unspoken words. "You don't have a choice. Neither of us do."

I close my eyes, both hating him and what he's doing to me. He leans back and tips my chin up with his fingers. My eyes slowly open and I'm surprised to find pity in his gaze.

"I promise you, angel. You're only mine." He searches my face looking for understanding or acceptance, but I'm sure he won't find either. I don't trust him, and I don't know what to believe. My breathing is still coming in short, shallow spurts, and my heart feels like it's in my throat. "They all know that. No one will touch you."

I try to come to terms with the fact that I'm going down there. Like this. With them.

"Just stay beside me, and keep quiet." He runs his thumb over my jaw until I meet his gaze. "You'll be safe with me, and if you listen, I won't have to punish you." Even with the fear of going down there, the idea of him punishing me sends a wave of want to my core.

I let out a heavy breath, and watch as Kade's eyes widen with lust and his lips kick up with a small smirk. He leans down and hesitates before taking my lips with his.

I cave at his comforting touch, leaning into him and needing some kind of reassurance. My lips soften against his as his fingers spear through my hair. My pussy heats, and I lean my body toward his.

Maybe we can just stay here. I can hide here and just be his.

As the thought enters my mind, Kade pulls away from me and I instantly miss his touch, and the soothing balm he gave me with it. As he moves away, my hands move up to grab him and keep him here, but I hesitate.

The sense of calm is completely gone, and I find myself moving closer to him.

"Don't leave me," I whisper as his hand rests on the doorknob. He turns around to look at me and I almost expect him to scold me for giving him a command, even though we both know it was a plea.

Instead he wraps a hand around my waist and plants a small kiss on my forehead.

"Never, angel. Just stay by my side."

❖ ❖ ❖

Kade opens the door and steps out. I follow him quickly, but I don't look up, keeping my eyes trained on the floor and that's where they're going to stay. Still, I can see the couple from before in my periphery. I can hear the sounds of her muffled moans and the man grunting and groaning as he pounds into her echoing in the hall. My heart races, and I nearly trip on Kade's feet.

"Angel," he says and gives me a low warning. I look up with wide eyes. He lays a hand on my head, letting it slowly smooth my hair. "Just relax."

I nod once because I can't speak. I just want to disappear. A few men in suits walk behind us at the top of the stairwell. I can feel their eyes on me, but I don't look up. I'll just look at the floor and try to stay next to Kade until he's done parading me around.

Fear and anxiety race through me, but I can't let them show. I'll be good. I just need to stay by his side. I feel as though I'm in imminent danger of being devoured, like I'm bleeding out in the middle of shark-infested waters and on death's door. And I know the only thing keeping me alive and safe right now is Kade. Yet he's the most dangerous predator there is.

As I follow him down the stairs, watching my feet and only my feet, I see several shiny, black shoes of men but also the small, bare feet of women walking the opposite direction, up the stairs. Women like me. My eyes slowly rise, and I'm nearly petrified to see a woman completely naked with rope wrapped around her throat and midsection.

I look at her eyes, but she doesn't look back. Her shoulders are squared, and her back straight. She walks with dignity, and it's then that I notice she's smiling and her hands aren't bound.

My lips part to ask a question and my head turns of its own accord and I nearly trip and fall down the stairs as Kade's grip on the leash pulls me forward. I nearly bump into his back as I catch my steps.

My heart beats faster with fear as several men around us turn to stare. Kade turns around and cocks a brow at me, as if daring me to say something.

The world around me stills as I look up at him. I'm lost and confused and scared. I just need him on my side.

"Do you need help, Master K?" I hear a man's voice offer to my right. My lungs stop, and I stare at Kade's shoes. My shoulders turn in and I want to run as the man steps closer.

I can feel him next to me. He chuckles and says, "She's new. And it looks like you've got your hands full."

"You'd like that, wouldn't you, Master A?" Kade says.

The man laughs and his fingers brush my shoulder, moving the hair to my back. My eyes widen with fear and I stare straight into Kade's eyes, but he's not looking at me. He's looking at the other man with a smile, as though everything is just fine.

My heart races faster when he turns to me and the smile falls. My body's paralyzed.

"She'll warm up soon enough," Kade says to the man, although he's still looking at me. The warmth on Kade's features still hasn't returned.

"I'm sure you'll do an excellent job with her," the man replies as a woman wearing a short, simple black dress passes behind him. She's balancing a silver tray in her hand carrying several champagne flutes filled with the sparkling liquid.

The man moves in my periphery, and I instinctively look at him.

He reaches out to the woman's tray and sets an empty glass on it. He's in a suit like Kade's but it's dark grey with a perfectly folded, bright white handkerchief in his pocket. He flashes the woman a dazzling, bright smile and shakes his head as she turns and lowers the tray for him to take a new glass.

"No thank you, love," he says with a boyish charm. The woman smiles and turns, leaving the man to look back at me. He has rich brown eyes and a classically handsome face that's freshly shaven.

"Say goodbye to Master A, Olivia," Kade says with a hint of admonishment in his voice, bringing me back to reality.

I open my mouth, but my throat is so dry, I have to swallow and clear it before I can say anything. I look up at the gorgeous man, and I can barely breathe. "Goodbye, Master A," I say in a rush as the words tumble from my mouth.

The man groans and pinches his forehead, looking at Kade as though I've just teased him. "You did that on purpose, you fucker." He says the words with humor in his voice.

Kade chuckles low and says, "You're an easy target."

Kade leans into me and asks loud enough for the man to hear, "Do you want him to be your Master?"

I quickly shake my head as fear grips my body.

Kade places a hand on my shoulder and rubs soothing circles on my body with his thumb. "Call him sir," he says simply.

"Sir." I'm quick to correct myself. I am not giving him permission to take me away from Kade. I have to actively resist the urge to cling to Kade.

"Say goodbye, *correctly*."

I look at the man who has a sad smile on his face. "Goodbye, sir."

"Goodbye, Olivia." He smirks and raises his brows with his hands in his pockets as he says, "You may change your mind later." He gives me a wink and looks back at Kade.

"Enjoy your night, Master K."

Kade nods and replies, "And you as well."

I expect Kade to start walking again, but he doesn't. Instead his eyes are focused on me, and I'm forced to look up at him.

His eyes flash with power and lust. He takes a step forward, and I'd take a step back, but I feel caught in his gaze and the steps are behind me.

"He'd love to have you, Olivia. They all would." His eyes travel my body with obvious appreciation. He licks his lips and then meets my gaze again. "You will call them sir, unless I tell you otherwise." He wraps the leash around his hand once, and then grips my chin in the same hand. His thumb rests gently on my lips.

"You did well, angel." With his words of approval he drops his hand, and tugs gently on the leash. I'm quick to follow, feeling as though I've passed some sort of test of his.

I don't want tests though. My feet continue to move as he leads me through a hall. My bare feet patter against the floor, but I can barely hear it. Dozens of people are talking and moving about. It's surreal. I try to breathe, but my body isn't cooperating. Kade leads me through a large set of dark wooden doors with intricate carvings, and the atmosphere seems to shift from lighthearted to something more dangerous and thrilling.

A sick feeling overwhelms me, but when I look up, awe replaces the negative emotions threatening to take over.

The room is like a ballroom. It reminds me of Beauty and the Beast in some respects, with large chandeliers and an expansive empty space with marble floors that shine in the dim light. But it's dark. So dark. There's faint music, but it's not the sweet classics they dance to in fairytales. The beats are low and dangerous. They're meant to entrance you.

The walls of the room are painted a dark grey, and the large floor-to-ceiling windows are draped with thick, dark red curtains. There's a large mahogany bar in between the two windows, and servers dressed in simple black pants with tight, white t-shirts. It takes a moment for my eyes to focus, but there are cages lining the back wall. They're large with a few square feet inside, and each one is nearly eight feet tall. With the low lighting it's almost hard to see the women dancing in the cages. The shimmer of their silver dresses catches my eye as they move in rhythm to the beat of the music.

In the cage closest to me, a woman's small hands are

wrapped around the bars, making her look even more delicate. Her eyes are closed, and she's lost in the music. Her hands move to her body, traveling up to her neck seductively, then to her hair. Her movements are sensual and mesmerizing. It's only when Kade takes a step forward and the chain pulls on my wrists do I realize I've been staring.

This room itself is a drug. It's intoxicating, frightening, and electrifying all at once. Had I stepped into this room by my own volition, I would sway my hips to the music. I would close my eyes and get lost in the divine pleasure this room crafts. It seems like most of the people are on the outskirts of the room, staying close to the walls and talking and drinking. They're hardly paying any attention to the stimulating sensations overwhelming me.

There are a good number of people, a few dozen at least, dancing in the center of the room. Some women are dressed in clubwear and heels, while others, like me, are in bare feet and barely any clothes at all. The sea of swaying hips and hands caressing bodies is accompanied with couples grinding against one another.

I fixate on a couple at the very edge. The man is in low-hung pants and he isn't wearing a shirt. He's holding his partner up with his hands on her ass, and her legs wrapped around his waist. Her head tilts back, and he kisses her neck as he pumps his arms up and down to the beat while she moves against him. My breathing comes in heavy pants as her lips part. They look so intimate that they must be fucking. But in a flash, they're lost in the crowd.

My feet don't stop moving as Kade tugs the chain around my wrists. He's wrapped the chain around his hand so much I'm forced to stay close to him. It's not until I hear the sounds of moaning and strangled cries that my feet stumble, and Kade's there to catch me, as though he anticipated my fall.

The music dies as we move away from the dance floor and closer to a thick curtain that divides the room in half. Guarding the area where the curtain splits are two tall muscular men, wearing the same black pants and tight white t-shirts as the bartenders. The curtain is made from the same deep red fabric as the ones covering the windows.

As we approach, I can hear several women's strangled cries, but I'm not certain if they're from pleasure, or pain. I grip onto Kade's side, my nails digging into his muscular back. He wraps an arm around me, but even as my feet refuse to work, he continues to push me to move.

My body is a confusing mix of fear and curiosity, jumbled up with arousal and anxiety.

I only move because I have to, and as I walk in Kade's embrace and see what lies in front of us, my blood runs cold.

Behind the curtain is a room of debauchery.

Anxiety races through my blood. I feel lost, just like Alice when she fell down the rabbit hole. There are multiple small areas separated by a thick, red rope, but each division is taken by a couple while spectators stand around watching. Some men are completely clothed, but a few have their pants undone and they're openly stroking their erect cocks.

I try not to stare as I see a man standing in front of a scene with a woman on her knees in front of him. Her head bobs up and down his length. On a small stage before them the woman is being taken by two men. The woman at the spectator's feet doesn't bother to look at the scene. Her one hand balancing herself on his thigh and her other stroking him. She eagerly takes him into her mouth as his hand spears through her hair and he looks between her and the woman in front of him.

"They want that, angel." I look up at Kade, scared and wanting to cling to him to save me. I want to plead with him not to leave me here. "They *asked* to be in this room." He tilts my head back so I'm forced to take in the room and this time I watch the scene playing out to my left.

The woman closest to me is completely naked and shackled to a bench. Her beautiful blonde hair is disheveled, but still partially pulled back in a ponytail.

I watch as her eyes close and she obeys her Master. He's standing in front of her, with his hands resting on her arms as another man grips her hips from behind and thrusts himself deep inside her. Sounds of pleasure spill from her mouth as she takes the relentless thrusts. Her mouth parts, and her body trembles. The man behind her groans and pulls away from her, cumming violently on her lower back.

I watch her Master.

His eyes never leave her face. Another man comes up behind her and forcefully pounds her, making her entire body jolt forward as he fucks her with a ruthless pace.

She gives a strangled cry and reaches out for her Master. He holds on to her, supporting her head in his hands. I watch as he kisses her passionately, capturing her cries with his lips.

His other hand runs along the curve of her waist, trailing down between the bench and her body. He keeps his eyes focused on hers as he rubs her clit.

"Cum, *esclave*. Show them how good you feel, *esclave*," he whispers into the space between them. She moans into his mouth and takes the punishing fuck from the stranger behind her. I'm entrapped in their passion; I've never seen anything like this before.

Kade pulls me away, and I refuse to look at the other scenes. I'm overwhelmed with my own varied emotions and concerns.

Does that woman even know who the man behind her is?

Does her Master? Has he given them permission ahead of time, or would he let anyone fuck her?

The questions race through my mind. But the truth is,

I'm not disgusted; I'm enthralled. My skin heats and tingles, and my pussy grows hot with need.

This is wrong. This is terrifying. But for a moment, it's intoxicating. The erotic thrill confuses me, and makes me genuinely afraid.

"Come, angel," Kade says as he pulls the chain tight on my wrists. "Your training starts tonight."

CHAPTER 12

Olivia

KADE LEADS ME THROUGH A NARROW HALLWAY and past a set of rooms. They're small, and each have a large square window that lets the people in the hallway see the entire room. There are small benches in the center of the hallway, but no one's sitting. A few windows have curtains pulled shut, but most are open so anyone can watch. I try not to look. I try not to listen to the sounds. But every one of my senses is flooded with sex. *Sex* is everywhere.

"You'll watch tonight," Kade says, stopping in front of a window.

His hands rest on my shoulders as I peer into the window and take in the scene. A redheaded woman with beautiful curls that drape down her back is turned away from us. A man stands to the left, circling her; he's appraising her.

His hand settles on her hip and he pulls her backward so her back hits his chest. His head lowers and he whispers something into her ear.

I want to ask Kade if everyone here is like... us. If she's forced to be there with him. She doesn't look it. Neither has anyone else. This isn't what I expected.

The woman in the room molds her body to his and nods, making her red locks bounce. I have so many questions. Kade told me to be quiet though. My heart sinks slightly. I resist the urge to turn in his arms and plead with him. I feel so lost and confused. I don't know anything.

The man leaves the woman standing with her back to us and approaches the window. He flicks a switch, and I hear a loud click.

"Tonight, my Sara will show her submission to me, and devotion to our lifestyle." He walks to the far edge of the room and picks up something off the floor. It's a paddle. My heart races faster in my chest. He's going to beat her!

My legs move naturally in an attempt to protest and

save her. My body heats. I can't stand by and watch this. *I won't.*

Kade's hands dig into my shoulders, forcing me to stay where I am. "He's not going to hurt her." He says the words simply, but I don't trust him. I don't believe him. A man to my left turns his head and stares at me. I almost look up at him and sneer, but Kade grips my chin and lowers his lips to my ear.

"You're being such a good girl, angel." His words make my body melt into his. I can't deny his approval makes me weak. "Just watch." He loosens his grip and takes my hips in his hands, keeping me in place.

"Kneel spread." The man gives a forceful command, but he also raises his hand and then lowers it with his fingers fanned out.

The woman drops to her knees and spreads her legs wide. I try to look away, but Kade holds the nape of my neck. I can see *everything*. Her ass rests on the heels of her feet, and her back is straight. I try not to look, but my eyes are drawn to her glistening sex. A violent heat floods my face as I blush. I search her face for anything, but she's completely neutral with her eyes on the floor.

"This position is excellent for display, but also for both punishment and reward due to the difficulty in maintaining the position, and the ease of access to her body, respectively." The man talks as he walks behind her. He sets the paddle down onto the bench and kneels next to her. He pinches her nipple and pulls outward. Her lips part slightly as her eyes close then slowly open, as she looks directly at his face.

"Good girl," he says as his hands roam her body while she remains perfectly still, giving him full control to do whatever he wishes.

As she stays still, he spreads her lips for us to see. Her nipples harden, and her breathing picks up as his fingers pump in and out of her. Once, twice, but after the third time he stops. Her body shudders as he moves his fingers to her clit. He stands and offers her his fingers, covered with her arousal.

"Suck," he commands, and before the word is even fully spoken, she takes them greedily into her mouth. She looks him in the eyes as she sucks and licks his fingers clean.

He smiles down at her and pets her hair before circling her body again and repeating the same routine again and again. Each time her legs seem to tremble more and more. Her breathing becomes ragged as she takes his fingers into her mouth. But she never finds her release. Instead he tells her to get into a different position, like the sitting position, which is exactly what I'd naturally assumed it would be.

I watch as she quickly moves from position to position

as he orders her to do. Most seem to make sense, like the first. But others I wouldn't expect. She knows each one perfectly though, and confidently maneuvers her body so she's on display for him however he's commanded.

What strikes me most is how at ease she is. She knows she won't be punished; the presence of the paddle, even as he smacks it in his hand, doesn't faze her in the least.

She stays in each position until told to resume a different position. I keep waiting for her eyes to catch mine. For some reason I need her to see that I'm watching. I feel as if I could tell she was okay, if only she would look at me. But she never does. Her eyes stay on the floor, or on her Master. Not once do they move to anyone else.

"Present down." As he says the words, his submissive lowers her body forward with her arms at her side. The man circles her once, but I can already tell something's wrong. His forehead is pinched, and his breathing quickens.

"You know this one, little bird. Are you doing this deliberately?" he asks her. It's the first time his voice has taken an edge of authority.

The woman lifts her head. A blush rises to her cheeks. "It's the last one," she says hesitantly.

He cocks a brow at her and crouches in front of her, but to one side so we can see her face. "Did you think you needed to fail one?" he asks.

She did it on purpose? My heart beats so loudly, it nearly drowns out all other sounds. I hear a rough chuckle from the man to my left. But I only faintly register it.

"I thought they should see the whip position," she whispers. He leans forward and takes her chin in his hand. He plants a quick kiss on her lips.

"Then get into position, my pet." She gives him a small smile and raises her ass in the air.

"My Sara deliberately disobeyed me. She also decided to top from the bottom." Sarah's body tenses on the ground. I don't know what his words mean, but I can at least tell she wasn't expecting them. "She will be properly punished."

He turns and picks up the wooden paddle off the bench.. He turns it over in his hands, examining it. He leans down and gently places it flat against her ass. He lifts it high and I close my eyes, waiting to hear a loud *smack*! But there's nothing. My body is tense. I slowly open my eyes and let out a shaky exhale.

Kade kneads my shoulders and says, "Relax, angel." His voice is soft and smooth.

I watch as the man pushes the handle of the paddle in and out of her pussy. I can't see everything, but I know that's what he's doing. His other hand is on her back, keeping her shoulders down and he's watching her face intently.

He withdrawals the paddle suddenly, and the submissive whimpers. "You'd be cumming by now if you'd done what you were supposed to do, Sara." He puts the handle of the paddle to his mouth and tastes her juices. Her eyes stay forward, unaware of what he's doing behind her. I watch as he unzips his pants and steps out of them, his large, erect cock on full display. He bends down behind her and runs the paddle along her spine, and over her ass.

My breathing picks up as I watch the man lift the paddle and then swing it down, hitting the woman's ass and leaving a bright red mark. Her head flies up and she screams out with obvious pain.

In a quick movement, the paddle slaps against her ass again. *Smack!* My body jumps as Sara lets out a wail. Again and again he swings the paddle. Her face is scrunched up and she tries to muffle her noises as he spanks her over and over.

My eyes refuse to close, and I struggle to breathe. My fists clench. *She knew this would happen,* I repeat to myself over and over. *It's okay. She knew.*

And then something changes. Her back arches, and she seems to greet the paddle invitingly, rather thanstruggling to stay in position. Her face relaxes, and she screams out a sound of pure pleasure.

Smack!

"Yes!" she screams, and I stand in shock.

Kade's arm wraps around my waist and he pulls me close to him so my back is pressed against his chest. I feel his hard erection digging into me at my back. My eyes close, and I swallow thickly as my nipples harden and arousal pools between my legs.

Intellectually, I'm confused with a range of emotions. But my body isn't. And it's betraying me.

Kade whispers in my ear, "That wasn't so bad, was it?"

The man gentles his hand on her ass, right on the bright red mark, and she winces. He shushes her and sets the paddle down on the bench again. He strokes his cock as he examines her ass. A moment passes in silence. "Present down, correctly this time!" her Master says.

Kade's hand slowly travels to my hip, pausing for a brief moment and then continues moving lower.

"Answer me, angel," Kade says in a smooth voice.

Other spectators gather around as the woman moves to her knees. She spreads them wider than the last time and lowers her upper body flat against the floor, her arms straight out and her palms up.

"No, Master K." The words fall from my lips as the man in the room settles on his knees behind the woman and lines his dick up at her opening. She rocks her pussy against him and moans before he's even touched her. He shoves himself inside of her and her head lifts with her mouth shaped in a perfect O. He thrusts behind her with an arm bracing her body. His other hand wraps around her throat, and he lowers his chest to her back.

"Good girl," he says as his pace picks up. His other hand

rubs her throbbing clit. He kisses her neck and nips her ear. "So fucking good," he breathes into her ear as he fucks her with a relentless pace.

Kade's own fingers travel to my heat. "Oh, angel," Kade groans as his fingers spread the moisture up to my clit. He kisses the tender spot behind my ear as the man grips the woman's hips and lifts her body off the floor to push deeper into her with each hard thrust.

I close my eyes as Kade's fingers dip into my soaking wet pussy.

Kade nips my ear and hisses an admonishment. "Open your eyes."

As the man fucks the woman bowed before him, Kade finger fucks me. Each thrust is perfectly in time with the scene before us.

"Yes!" the woman screams out, then bites her lip to quiet her moans of pleasure as her body rocks with each powerful movement from the man behind her. His hand grips her hip and smacks her ass as he mercilessly fucks her.

My own body leans forward as my body heats and my legs tremble. My pussy clenches around Kade's fingers, and I struggle to contain my silent scream. Arousal leaks down my leg as my pussy spasms around his fingers with my own orgasm.

I look up, barely able to catch my breath and find the woman panting on the floor.

The man stands with their combined cum on his cock. He grabs a blanket from a nearby shelf and covers her before lifting her into his arms and kissing her on the lips. Kade turns me in his arms and starts leading me away.

My legs hardly function and I try to lean against him as my eyes threaten to close.

"Not yet, angel," Kade says and kisses my hair. "You need to walk back to the room on your own. I can't carry you yet."

CHAPTER 13

Olivia

I STARE AT THE CHAINS ON THE FLOOR NEXT TO a large floor pillow. It's time to sleep. And apparently, I'll be sleeping on the floor.

"Do I need to use the restraints?" Kade asks. I feel numb looking at the chains bolted to the floor. They're such a contrast. The room is spacious and luxurious, yet it's designed to be a prison. "If you killed me, you'd have to go out there with them."

My eyes slowly find Kade's as I say, "I don't want to kill you." *Kill him?* I'm so confused by everything. I don't know what to think anymore. My heart sinks in my chest.

"Until you submit to me, I think it's best you sleep here." Kade gestures to the large pillow on the floor. It's long enough that my body will fit however I want to lay, but it's not a bed. I part my lips to ask him what it means to submit to him so I can sleep on a real bed, but then I slam them shut. I know what it means, and that's not happening. My anger is short-lived as I stare at the bed.

My heart slowly falls and I nod my head and slowly lower my body to the floor.

"Tomorrow, I'll get you ready before training." My shoulders hunch forward. Every step back to the room was a step back to reality and away from the fantasy I'd conjured in my head. I breathe out deeply, trying to maintain my composure.

"Yes, Master K." I keep my eyes on the floor pillow, my fucking bed until I'm able to get the fuck out of here.

"You can call me Kade here, Olivia." His voice is soft, and I hear him just fine, but I can't give him a verbal response. So instead I just nod my head.

"Go to sleep, angel." With a loud click, Kade locks the doors and turns off the lights. A faint stream filters through the room from under the door. It gives me just enough light that I can see him lift his shirt over his head and drop his pants to the floor.

The bed groans as he climbs in and gets under the sheets.

It's better this way. I can sleep here, and I can do as I'm told until I can figure out some sort of escape.

I take in a deep breath and try to calm myself. This is temporary. I can fine a way out of this. I tell myself over and over, but I know it's false. My chest aches, and my throat closes. I know it's not true. I just don't want to admit it to myself.

I hear the faint music and soft laughter. Occasionally there are footsteps. Some are close to the door. I lie on the pillow facing the door, but I can't breathe.

I try to sleep for maybe hours, I don't know. But every time I hear the steps come close to our door I jump, and the fear keeps me wide awake.

"Angel." My body tenses as Kade's voice pierces through the night.

"Y-Yes, Master—" I try to speak. I can't begin to know why I'm so emotional. Why now of all times, I'm struggling.

He climbs off the bed and comes for me. My initial thought is to push him away, or to run from him. To hit him.

But I do nothing. Instead I let him lift me into his arms and carry me into the large bed.

He covers both of us with the blankets and pulls my naked body toward him. "Hush, angel."

I close my eyes, waiting for him to use me however he wants. I can't fight anymore. Not here. I feel helpless. Like the illusion of freedom has been ripped away from me.

"It's alright." He kisses my shoulder and settles in behind me, splaying his hand on my belly. "Go to sleep now. You're safe."

My body relaxes slightly, but I don't believe him. I wait with my eyes open. But the only movement he makes is to gently stroke my hair with his other hand.

My eyes feel heavy, and the part of me that's stopped fighting takes over.

I lean against Kade and fall into a deep sleep.

Dreaming of cages and whips, chains and collars. The images flash before my eyes. I feel his hands on me and I enjoy every second. I hear the sounds of the whips and I arch my back, welcoming the exotic feel.

I wake with my heart pounding and my pussy clenching in the middle of the night. It's dark, with only faint bits of light from the moon filtering in through the curtain. I search the room, but there's nothing. Only Kade behind me, holding me close to him.

For a second I think I should run. I should leave him.

But then I hear footsteps in the hall. Heavy ones.

I settle back into Kade's embrace.

Bringing me here was deceitful. He's forced me to look at him as a savior rather than my captor. I can't forget who he really is. No matter how much I'm starting to crave his touch and this darkness he's introduced me to.

CHAPTER 14

Olivia

I WAKE UP TO THE BRIGHT LIGHT AND INSTANTLY bolt upright. I pull the covers around my naked body and slowly take in the room. I'm flooded with the memory of the night before, and my heart races frantically. A shiver runs through my body as I realize it's all true. It wasn't a nightmare or a depraved fantasy.

This is real.

The door cracks open and I turn sharply, watching

Kade enter with a plate balanced on his hand. He closes the door behind him and keeps his eyes on me as he walks to the bed. I slowly scoot away until my back is pressed to the headboard, and I pull the blanket tighter around myself.

"Whenever I come in, you will greet me appropriately," he says with his icy blue eyes staring straight into mine. The comforting touch of last night is gone, and in its place is absolute authority.

A lump grows in my throat and I try to respond, but my voice croaks. I bow my head slightly and ball the blanket in my hands. I cower, like a pathetic little bitch.

"It's alright, angel. I haven't taught you yet." He's calm in his response and he climbs on the bed. He sits next to me and gently pulls the blanket away as though that's just fine. It is to him.

He owns me.

"You need to bow and keep your eyes lowered to the floor until I address you." He splays his hand across my back and pushes me forward. I let him move my body into a bow. I know the position from last night's lesson.

"And don't ever hide your body from me." I close my eyes and stay still as the bed dips and he moves away.

"That's better."

I slowly open my eyes as his hand cups my chin. He tilts

my head up and runs his thumb along my lower lip. "You're doing so well, Olivia. You have no idea."

Again his approval makes my tense body ease with slight comfort.

"I've seen a lot of training, and you would make an excellent example for all of them."

My heart sinks and I pull away from his hand, hating that he's touching me at all. *How many women is a lot?* Anxiety, fear, and disgust all overwhelm me in a minute.

"Angel," he says with a threatening tone. My body stills and my heart slows. "You cannot move away from me. Do you understand?"

I nod my head once and let out a small, "Yes." I can feel his eyes on me, but I don't look up at him. I can't.

"What's bothering you?" he asks after a moment. My blood heats, and I bite my tongue. Is he fucking serious?

"When I ask you a question, you will answer it." Kade's voice is hard and I want to snap at him in return. But I clench my teeth and finally look up and respond by asking, "What happened to the others you trained?"

"Once they're trained, they're given to their owners." There's no remorse in his voice. He must sense my disgust though because he adds, "I know the ones I've trained have enjoyed their positions, angel. It's not all the horrors you've conjured in your head."

"Will you sell me?" I ask before I lose my nerve. I have to know.

"No," he's quick to respond, and I stare back at him with apprehension. *He's lying to me.*

"You're mine, and only mine." Something about the conviction in his voice eases a pain deep inside of me. I feel my defenses fall, and my armor seems to chip.

But I don't want to be owned. Not by him; not by anyone.

Kade pulls me closer to him. His hands grip my hips as he settles me in his lap. I'm tense and completely naked, yet he's fully clothed.

"I'll make you a deal, angel." Kade reaches to the plate sitting on the end of the bed and grabs a small slice of strawberry before he commands, "Open your mouth." I stare at his fingers for a moment, but then I obey.

I'll save my fight for when I truly need it. Right now I'll bide my time and play along with this shit.

I part my lips and let his thick fingers slip the small bit of fruit into my mouth. I close my eyes and practically moan at the sweet taste. It's only then that I realize how hungry I am. I haven't eaten in over a day.

"You do as I say," Kade instructs and reaches for another piece while I eagerly wait for him to bring it to my lips. "You show them that I can create the perfect slave, and I'll give you your freedom." He pushes the fruit into my mouth, but I can't chew. My body feels frozen.

He'll give me my freedom. Lies! He must be lying to me.

"Until then, I'll give you everything you need. I'll keep you safe, and you'll obey me." I have to work hard to keep my hands from fisting. I'm not going to willingly roll over and let him fuck me. But he hasn't tried yet. He could have, but he hasn't.

"How does that sound, angel?" he asks as I finally chew and swallow the small piece.

"It sounds like a lie." The words tumble out of my mouth without my permission. My eyes fly to his and widen with fear.

Much to my surprise, the corners of his lips pull up into an asymmetric grin. "I won't lie to you." He purses his lips for a moment and then adds, "Things aren't quite what they seem to be."

I don't get his cryptic meaning, but I'm also not interested. I don't believe he'll let me go. Not for one second.

"I can't tell you much, but I can tell you that very shortly, I'll be traveling soon. I won't be in the U.S., and if I sent you on your way back home, you'd be safe and I'd be safe from prosecution." He brings a slice of orange to my mouth and I have to open my lips wider. I take in the succulent slice and hold his eyes.

"I don't have a need for you where I'm going, and I won't mind sending you back home." I search his eyes and his face, but he seems sincere.

"I need you right now though." He looks away and his hand hovers over the plate before deciding on another slice of orange. For the first time, I see a sliver of vulnerability from him.

"I need you to be perfect for me, and then I can leave and you can go home."

I want to ask him what he means. I need a concrete answer and plan, but I already know he won't tell me.

"You can't tell anyone I offered you this deal, my sweet angel." I nod my head and swallow before promising, "I won't."

He gives me a small smile, but it's sad. He cups my chin in his hand and leans forward and whispers, "They'll kill me and most likely you."

My heart lurches in my chest. "I shouldn't have said anything, but I'm truly sorry you're in this situation." I look up into his eyes and I believe him. I may be naïve or stupid, but I do.

"So just be quiet and be good for me, and everything will be alright."

I nod my head and say, "I will." I speak the truth.

"Olivia," he says firmly, "don't ever speak of this again. Not to me; not to anyone."

I nod my head and let the fear of what would happen wash over me.

CHAPTER 15

Olivia

"KNEEL." KADE'S VOICE IS CALM, AND I'M QUICK to sit down on my heels. My legs are firmly pressed together. My back is straight, and I keep my eyes forward. I've had days of practice. I know these positions by heart now. It's easy to listen and obey these commands. They're all I've done, and thankfully, all that Kade has asked from me. I've obeyed everything without question, only thinking about being set free.

He leans down and gently brushes my nipples with the backs of his fingers.

My pussy clenches, and my nipples harden at his touch. This is a part of training, but I'm not giving in to him or his touch. I can't let myself be fooled. I'll play the part and do what I have to do to survive. But that's all this is. It's just me surviving until I can get out of here.

"Spread," he says in a low voice.

My knees move to the side, exposing myself to him. My heart races faster, but I do my best not to show it.

"Good girl," he barely speaks above a murmur. My lips part with his approval. I almost said thank you. Before I can think too much on my thoughts and the effect his approval has on me, I hear a zipper. The sound fills the room. I don't look up, but I don't have to. Kade's pants drop to the floor in a crumpled heap. The belt smacks the floor with a clank and I watch as he steps out of them.

"Look at me, angel." My eyes raise to his. They beg me to look straight ahead. His cock is right there, proud and large. Precum is already glistening at the head.

My breathing comes in frantic pants. "This is something they'll want to see."

I nod my head once. I knew this was going to happen eventually. I slowly open my mouth for him. But he doesn't move. I'd rather just get this over with. A moment passes and I hesitantly look up at him.

"Stay," he says. And with that simple command he leaves the room.

I close my mouth and finally breathe. My body sags forward and I want to collapse on the ground, but I don't. I need to be in this position when he returns.

I don't know how long we've been in this room, but it feels like forever. It's nearly empty and nothing like the bedroom.

This room was made for training. The walls and floor are cement. Neither are painted, and it gives a grim atmosphere. That, combined with the tools on the back wall and machines in the room makes it feel like a room designed for torture, although Kade informed me otherwise.

They can be used for pleasure, angel. "Can" being the operative word.

I could try to kill him. The thought sneaks into the crevice of my mind. There are paddles and whips and other tools of the trade at my disposal. I could grab one and try to overpower him. If I hit him just right when he walked back in, maybe I would be able to kill him or at least knock him unconscious.

But then what? I'd have to sneak up the stairs and try to find my way out without anyone noticing. And then run? I don't even know where I am, or what's outside. And I'm completely naked.

There are so many fucking people here. Men I've never met all know my name.

And if they found me running...

Kade said he'd give me my freedom. He said he'd protect me from them, and he'd be the only one to touch me.

And I believe him. I tear my eyes away from the back wall and concentrate on the concrete floor.

As horrid as this room is, I can't deny I'm turned on. It's Kade—his hands, his voice, his authority. Everything about him turns me on.

Every time I got into a position, he'd move me slightly. His firm grip would spread my legs wider, and then they'd linger on my body. Every touch was like a jolt of electricity. But I've done my best to keep my mind on the training.

I just need to do this right, and then I can leave.

As the thought hits me, the door opens and I quickly move back to the right position. I stay perfectly still and stare at the ground.

I hear Kade's footsteps, but then the faint pitter-patter of bare feet.

I have to seriously resist the urge to look up and see who else is with him. But I don't have to wonder for too long.

"Talia, kneel in front of my angel." Kade sounds confident and sure of himself.

I lift my eyes but not my head as the beautiful woman displays herself in front of me. At least she's wearing a dress. Our knees touch for a moment and then she sits back on her heels.

He brought in someone else.

I remember her from the first night. Anxiety races through my blood. I have to blink back my tears.

"Talia," Kade says, "Olivia has been a very good girl. I'd like you to comfort her."

I watch Talia cautiously as she reaches out to me and gently places her hand over mine. My body tenses at her soft touch.

My heart races, and I look up at Kade. I don't understand, but I don't like this. I don't know why he brought her in here, and I sure as shit don't need her comforting me.

Talia takes my hands in hers and gently rubs circles on the backs. "It's alright, Olivia. You're doing so well." It's the first time I've heard Talia's voice. It's low and soft, but also soothing. "He's so very proud of you." My eyes reach hers and my brow furrows. I don't like that she knows anything about us. Her eyes flash with fear as she takes in my expression, and her smooth motions falter.

Her lips part and then close, and she clears her throat before looking up to Kade. "I don't know how, Master K."

Master K. I remember how Kade said to call the other

men sir. That calling them Master meant you wanted to be theirs. The memories of that night flash before my eyes. Those men who fucked her that night. Did she call them all Master? Anger slowly courses through my blood, at her and then at this situation. At Kade.

But mostly because I'm fucking jealous. She's staring up at Kade, a man I'm trying to keep at bay, and she wants him. I know she does.

I'm fucked up in the head for being jealous, but I am.

I rip my hands away from hers and scoot back so that my back hits the wall behind me and I pull my legs into my chest.

He brought her in here to hurt me. That fucking bastard.

"Angel?" Kade says my pet name, but I ignore him. I can't respond right now. I've worked so hard to be *good*. I was even going to suck him off! Tears prick my eyes. I was going to be his good slave, and he brought in another because why? I didn't move fast enough for him?

"What's wrong, Olivia?" Kade asks, but his voice is stern.

"Did I hurt you?" Talia asks with sincerity.

"Yes," I croak out and harshly wipe at the unshed tears before they have a chance to show themselves. *Try to be good. Earn your freedom.* Somewhere these thoughts are in the back of my mind, but *fuck them both* is the voice that takes over.

"Why don't you just take her if you want her?" I sneer at Kade. My eyes snap to his, and I instantly regret the decision.

His eyes narrow and heat with anger. Talia's eyes go wide and she folds in on herself, bowing and lowering her head to the floor. She's completely submitted.

My heart races as Kade's hand whips down and grips my mouth. My heart beats frantically in my chest.

Stupid! Stupid! What the fuck is wrong with me? Fuck! My breathing falters.

"You will apologize to me and to Talia, or you will be punished." Kade's voice is low and threatening. He rips his hand away with such force that I nearly topple over.

"I'm sorry." I'm quick to spit out the words as my palms smack against the concrete and I brace my body and move into a bow like Talia. "I'm sorry, Master K. I'm sorry, Talia." I mimic her position as perfectly as I can.

Blood rushes in my ears as I watch Kade pace the room. His hand runs through his hair with frustration.

"I didn't bring her in here for me. I brought her in here for you!"

I can hardly believe what he's saying. What the fuck was he thinking? A long moment passes, and finally I hear Kade drag a chair across the room. The feet scratch against the concrete until he moves it directly between Talia and me.

"Talia, do you enjoy getting off?" Kade asks. My heart races faster. I'll never forgive him if he touches her. Never.

"I do." Talia's answer is simple.

"Do you want to help me train angel?" he asks and quickly adds, "It would please me if you would."

"I do, Master K." Talia uses his name again, but the anger hardly registers this time. My mind races with possibilities.

"Talia, kiss my angel." Kade gives the command, and I tense.

Talia rises, her blonde hair swinging in front of her shoulders. She crawls over to me and gentles her hand on my back, peting my hair before leaning down and kissing my forehead. Her lips are soft, and the motion is over quickly. It's almost like a mother kissing her child good night.

But I don't see the point.

Kade stands and walks to the shelf in the back of the room. He comes back with what looks to be a microphone at first, but it's not. It's a huge ass vibrator.

"Thank you Talia, but that's not going to work." Kade sets the vibrator on a low speed, and I can hear it humming as it comes to life.

"Lean back and pleasure yourself," Kade says as he holds out the vibrator but doesn't give it to her as she tries to take it. "But don't you dare cum until you're permitted to," he says before letting her accept it.

Talia nods her head once and obediently says, "I under-stand."

She pulls her dress up slightly and lies on the floor with her legs spread. She isn't facing either of us, so I can't see her pussy and I'm grateful for that.

She lets out a low moan and starts moving the vibrator against her clit in slow circles.

"This can be pleasurable." Kade moves to the ground next to me. "There's no shame in enjoying this."

I try to stay still as his arm wraps around my waist. "Watch her, angel." I swallow thickly and look straight ahead. Talia's pebbled nipples show through the thin mate-rial of her dress. Her eyes are almost closed, and her lips are parted as she takes shallow breaths.

She bites down on her bottom lip and her legs snap back as she pulls the vibrator away from her clit. Her eyes open and she looks to Kade. "May I cum, Master K?" she asks with desperation.

The sight of her on edge makes my body heat.

"Ask my Olivia." Kade's words make my heart race. What the fuck?

"Mistress, please, may I cum?" Talia's blue eyes hold my gaze.

"Yes," I answer quickly and then look up at Kade, but he scolds me.

"Keep your eyes on her." His words are hard.

I grip my fingers in my lap and watch as Talia rocks her hips in motion with the vibrator. It doesn't take long before her back bows and she lets out a soft cry as her orgasm shoots through her body.

She starts to set the vibrator down, but Kade stops her with a firm, "No."

She doesn't hesitate to move the vibrator back to her heat. Her brow furrows, and her head thrashes. She's already primed for another.

"Please, Mistress," she begs me.

"Yes," I say and turn toward Kade. "Can she please stop?" I ask him.

I feel hot all over. And I can't help that the sight of her own orgasm turns me on. I have no interest in her whatsoever, but the sight of her finding her pleasure is tantalizing.

"If you'd like," Kade replies simply.

I nod my head and watch as Talia cums again. Her eyelids flutter, and her legs shake as she finds her second release. She gently lays the vibrator on the floor and rises to the waiting position. Her skin is flushed, and her hands tremble slightly.

"Good girl, Olivia." I look up at Kade with confusion. "Would you like Talia or me to give you your reward?" he asks, and I look between the two of them, not knowing what to say.

My mouth opens and closes. I hesitate. We've been over

this, and hesitation isn't okay. I need to respond. With anxiety shooting through me, I answer, "You."

Kade gives me a stunning smiles and nods his head.

"Lie back then, angel."

Nearly numb, I gently lower myself to the floor. Talia's eyes are trained on the ground, somewhat giving us privacy. My cheeks heat with a violent blush.

"Grab your knees so I can see you better." I do as I'm told and pull my knees back, exposing my glistening sex. I'm so turned on and desperate for a release, but it still feels wrong.

"You enjoyed watching her before." Kade talks as he pushes my legs open even farther. The cool air touches my heat and makes me even more aware of how ready I am.

"I thought maybe it was Talia." He pushes two fingers into my hot, wet pussy. My mouth parts and my back bows as he strokes my G-spot and presses his thumb against my clit.

"I would have given you as many women as you wanted," he says as he pumps his fingers in and out of me. A strangled cry leaves my lips. As I turn my head to the side, I see Talia watching. Her fingers dig into her thighs and she's practically panting as she watches Kade finger fuck me.

Her eyes widen as Kade's head lowers and he takes a languid lick of my pussy.

"But it wasn't her, was it?" Kade asks before blowing

on my clit. The chill makes my legs shake with the need to cum. I'm so close.

"No," I answer without thinking.

"No, it was how the men fucked her one after the other." My pussy clenches around his fingers, and I cum. I hold my breath and close my eyes as my body trembles. Waves of pleasure move from my core and shoot outward.

"Oh," a deep voice says from behind me. I whip my head up to look at the door. It's open, and Gabriel is standing there. I'm still on my back, naked and because of that he's upside down. I'm quick to look back down at Kade.

Fuck! I swallow hard and wish I could disappear.

"Well, if you ever need help..." A shudder runs through my body at his words. I want to close my eyes, but Kade's gaze is holding me. I'm trapped in the heated look he's giving me.

"I didn't plan on sharing," he says with his eyes still on me. I hear Gabriel's shoes smacking against the concrete as he walks over to Talia. Kade finally looks up to Gabriel, and he clenches his jaw and adds, "But then again, I didn't think she'd want that."

Gabriel chuckles as he pets Talia's hair.

"Come *esclave*, I need you." He holds his hand down and she slips her small hand in his. She's graceful to stand, but her legs are still shaky. He gives her a warm smile and puts his arm behind her back, wrapping it around her waist.

I turn to look away as he moves his gaze to me. I want to cover my body since I'm naked and I don't want him staring at me, but I don't. I can't. That's not allowed.

I only breathe once the door clicks closed.

"How do you feel, angel?" Kade asks as he scoops my body into his arms. He holds me against his chest and sits back in the chair.

How do I feel? Confused, scared, *aroused*. I'm tired because I've barely been able to sleep on that damn pillow. The first night I finally slept with him holding me in bed. But he hasn't brought me back to bed with him since. He's asked me every night, but I refuse.

"I don't know," I answer honestly. It feels like there's a hard lump in my chest. It's pressing against my heart and making everything uncomfortable.

A small voice inside my head is whispering to just let go. That if I stop fighting and just put my faith in Kade, everything would be easier. *It would be. Everything would be easier.* But then I'd lose myself. I can already feel that I'm on the brink of a steep cliff. If I fall, I'd shatter at the bottom, completely beyond repair.

I move my hand to my throat and tilt my head into Kade's chest.

He's so warm, so strong. What's worse is I feel safe with him. I don't feel on edge. It's not how I thought it would be. He's in complete control, and there's no doubt in my mind

I have to listen to him for my very survival. But the commands are few, and mostly common sense.

Kade takes a deep inhale and I look up into his eyes. I can see he wants to say something, but instead he leans down and he kisses me.

His lips press against mine. His tongue glides against the seam of my lips and I part them. His hand splays across my back and he pushes me closer to him. My breasts press against his chest. He moans into my mouth. I can feel his hard dick pressing into my ass.

And I want it. I want *him*. As sick as it may be, desire stirs low in my core.

His power may arouse me, but it's this side of him that makes my defenses crash hard around me. His soft touch makes me weak. It threatens to destroy my very being.

He pulls away from me and I slowly open my eyes. My breathing is ragged, and my skin hot. "Not yet, angel. Not yet."

CHAPTER 16

Olivia

I HEAR THE DOORKNOB CLICK AND IT'S ENOUGH to wake me. My eyelids open as I hear the door creak open. I move quickly to get on my knees and kneel for Kade. I can't help the yawn, but luckily my face is down so I doubt he can even tell.

I don't think he'd mind much if he did see. Kade doesn't seem to mind much at all, really. He's held up his end of the deal. I behave, and he teaches me how to be a good slave. A shudder runs through my body as I think the word. *Slave.* I'm not much of a slave though. Not in the way I thought. He rewards me when I'm good, which is every day. I don't have a chance to run, and I'm not going to push him until I have that chance.

Instead it seems like I'm watching everything from afar. Like I'm not really here. It's not really me that he commands, *Spread yourself for me.* My body obeys, but in my mind I'm simply surviving. It's not my body that he lights aflame with desire. When he pushes his fingers inside of me and tells me to beg him to let me cum, I'm only doing what I need to do. Even if I enjoy it. Even if I crave it. I can't deny that I look forward to him touching me. I love seeing the desire and lust flicker in his eyes. His hands on my body are like a drug. Every day that passes I have to remind myself this is all just an act. *Isn't it?*

But it feels so good. I can't deny how I look forward to it now. With every position that exposes me to him, he makes me cum over and over.

He hasn't made me do anything to him though. I know it's coming. It has to be. That's the point of what I am. Still, he hasn't even hinted at it. It's almost like that first day he pulled out his cock never happened. At times I felt him on me and my body pushes me to give him pleasure, but I can't. I have to wait for his command. I'm eager for it as I wait on edge for my own release.

But then training ends and I seem to remember everything. It's like a switch. Only now I don't much fear the darkness.

Kade's hand gentles on my head and I know that means I can get up, but I don't want to. I'm tired. I've been sleeping on this damn pillow every night to stay away from him as best I can. My body is pleading with me to sleep in bed with him. To beg him. But I don't want to risk it. If I lie next to him, I'll want more. And so will he.

I pull my body up and look into his soft blue eyes. My core heats, and I'm already growing wet for him. He did that. He trained me to be this way. "I need you to be a good girl while I get ready for dinner. I'm taking you downstairs."

My heart races, and I'm instantly awake. I haven't been anywhere other than the training room and the bedroom for however long it's been. Maybe a week now? No, longer. I'm not sure.

I nod my head, keeping my eyes on his although apprehension races through me.

"I got you something to wear tonight," he says and smirks at me, "but I want you in it now." My heart speeds up. I have no idea what he means. When we're alone, I'm naked. Maybe it's a collar or cuffs. Nothing else. Outside of this bedroom, I wear what he tells me to. Which is usually a short thin dress.

"Get on the bed, Olivia." The way he says those words makes my pussy clench.

I sit on my knees with him behind me.

He shows me the wide, black leather collar with several silver loops on it. It's new. He fastens it to my neck, the smooth leather gently sliding across my tender skin until it's in place. I stay still as he attaches a thick silver chain to the back of it. My hair tickles my shoulders as he lifts it out of the way. It's a leash.

He bucks his hips into my ass and I slide forward on the bed with a small gasp. His hard dick is still pressed against my pussy. Only the thick fabric of his pants is between us. Shamefully, I feel myself heat for him. I want him. I want to know what it's like. He tempts and teases me every day and night, never taking from me.

My hands slip across the soft sheets, and the cold chain lifts from my back but before I can bow completely, he pulls the chain and I'm pulled back slightly by the collar around my neck. It tightens, but not to the point of pain or limiting my breath. I stay exactly how he has me positioned, my back arched and my fingers digging into the mattress to support this pose.

I hear him groan in satisfaction as his fingers gently glide down my waist, hip and then thigh, leaving goosebumps along the way. He shifts behind me and a chill runs up and down my spine. I hear the chain fall before I feel the cold metal on my back. He lays it down against my spine with care and then over my ass, letting the remainder pool between my legs and onto the mattress.

He splays a hand on my lower back while his other cups my pussy. I close my eyes in shame, knowing just how hot and wet I am for him.

"You're such a good girl, angel." He bends down and plants a kiss on my lower back. He moves the long chain between my pussy lips and up my stomach. I hear the clinking as he threads it through one of the silver loops in the collar and then tightens it.

My lips part with a gasp as the cold metal presses against my throbbing clit.

"Stay," he commands me and I obey. The bed dips, and I resist the urge to turn and look as he opens and then quickly closes a dresser drawer.

He moves back behind me and settles a hand on my lower back.

My forehead pinches as he slips an egg-shaped device into my slick pussy. It has a curve on the end that just barely touches my clit and bumps up against the chains. If I'm still, there's hardly any sensation, but the slightest movement feels so intense. Every nerve ending is on edge and ready to explode. I'm already primed from the training session today.

"Be a good girl and keep this in while I get ready." He starts to leave, but then he asks, "Do I need to chain you? I don't want you to move at all."

"No, Kade," I answer quickly. I almost said Master. I almost forgot we're in the bedroom.

"I mean it, angel. Be a good girl and just enjoy this." I turn slightly to meet his eyes as he clicks a button on a remote.

My mouth opens with a gasp and my body almost collapses as the device starts to vibrate in my pussy and against the thick chains. The humming movement of the chain makes my body heat, and pleasure stir within my lower belly. I drop my head to the mattress and moan into the sheets.

I'm on edge and dying for a release within seconds.

I lift my head to plead with him to make it stop or to give me more, I'm not sure which one. But he's not here. As my toes curl and the pleasure rises, the urge to grind against the chains is strong.

I moan Kade's name with desperation.

But he's already gone.

CHAPTER 17

Kade

I DON'T THINK I'VE EVER SHOWERED SO QUICKLY in my life. I spent more time jerking off than anything else. I've had to ease my baser needs myself. I can't be hard around Olivia. I want to fuck her every second of every day, but she's not ready for that. I can't take advantage of my sweet angel. She's trying so hard, and doing so well. I only need them to see how good she is. She can do this. She's still holding back, but she trusts me. She's even turned on by being my pet.

I'm a sick bastard for enjoying this as much as I am.

Fucking her would only condemn me further. It's going to happen. It *has* to happen. But I want her to truly desire it.

I could hear her moaning and panting the second I walked away.

I smile slowly as I dry my hair with the towel. I heard her cum more than once while I stroked myself off in the shower. Even over the pounding of the water splashing against the tile.

I've memorized the way she bites down on the tip of her tongue when it gets too much for her body to handle. When she explodes with pleasure and her head falls back, each time it's because of me. I give her that pleasure. I want to give her more. I need to feel her pussy spasming around my cock and not my hand.

It's wrong, but I want it. I desperately need to fuck her.

Fuck! I'm rock hard again. Just the thought of Olivia makes me ache for her. Every day she submits to me more and more easily drives me to take her.

She'd let me. I know she would. All I'd have to do is ask. But I don't know if it's because she's just trying to survive, or if she truly wants me. In the heat of the moment, she'd give me anything I asked of her. The beast inside me wants to reward her as a Master should.

Instead I'm being a pussy about it all. This *needs* to

happen. I won't be able to save her otherwise. My hands fly to my hair and grip tightly in frustration. I need to take this to the next step, but it'll solidify something I don't want.

I wish it didn't have to be like this.

I know they'll be here soon. Gabriel's told me they've called more than once to see how she's doing. I clench my jaw hating how they even know about her.

But that's the reason she's here. I can't forget that. Yet it constantly slips my mind. I'm ashamed that I keep forgetting. The thoughts of everything I've been through, of everything that's been sacrificed, thoughts of James fill my head and I'm quick to shut it all down. I don't want to think about it.

I hear her soft moans and I'm drawn to them. She's a beautiful distraction and so much more.

I drop the towel and open the bathroom door.

I walk out slowly, and look at my angel; my dick stands at full attention when I see her.

Olivia's on all fours with her ass raised high in the air, just how I left her. I circle the bed and see her hand is holding the vibrator in place. Her arousal's leaking down her thighs and her entire body is trembling. Without her holding it in, it would have easily fallen out.

"Please," she begs me.

"Please what, angel?" I ask her calmly, at complete odds

with her desperation. I know what she needs. I should replace that vibrator with my dick. That's what we both need.

"Please," she moans louder with her forehead scrunched. She doesn't want to beg me to fuck her. She simply doesn't want it badly enough. She doesn't want *me*. My heart squeezes painfully in my chest, but I don't give myself time to think about it.

I climb on the bed and ignore my desire to push my dick into her hot cunt. Fuck, I want her. I want her more than anything else. As my hand settles on her lower back, she moves her hand away and steadies herself on the bed, raising her hips so I can take care of her needs.

I gently pull the vibrator out of her heat. She's so wet and hot. I watch as her pussy clenches around nothing, and I have to close my eyes.

She's *mine*. She was given to me. And she agreed to be my slave as long as I set her free when I can.

Mine. Mine to do with as I please. I grip my cock in my hand and slowly open my eyes. She's fucking gorgeous. Her cheek is pressed to the mattress, and she looks back at me with half-lidded eyes. Her skin is smooth and flushed.

"Tell me what you want angel." I barely speak the words. My heart hammers in my chest. She turns her head away from me and takes in an unsteady breath. I can hear the words begging to be spilled from her lips. But she doesn't say them. She lets out a long exhale with her eyes closed tight. "Please," she whimpers.

I push two fingers into her hot cunt and stroke against her G-spot with my thumb pressing down on her clit. I'm fighting against my desire and it's a hard battle to win. It doesn't take more than a few pumps until she's cumming. I feel her pussy pulse around my fingers and groan. My dick leaks with the need to be inside her. My heart pounds in my chest.

Her head tilts up, and she lets out the sexiest moan with her eyes barely closed.

I pull away from her quickly, before I do anything stupid.

I'll hold her in a minute. I'll give her the aftercare she needs.

But first I need a release.

When I get to the bathroom, I close the door and lean my back against it.

My breathing is frantic as I wipe my brow with the back of my hand.

I fucking want her. This is a dangerous game I'm playing. I'm in too deep. But all I want is her.

CHAPTER 18

Olivia

IT'S BEEN DAYS SINCE I'VE REALLY SEEN ANYONE
else. I feel protected with Kade. When he takes me to the
training room I know other people are here. I can see them
in my periphery as Kade leads me through the house. But
I keep my eyes down. Sometimes I hear them talking.
Occasionally Kade stops to talk to them.

I've seen Master A more than a few times. He seems to

be very close to Kade. Almost as close as Gabriel. I've talked to them a few times. As in, I've said hello and thank you.

Whenever I see anyone other than Kade, it's only in passing, and nothing like this.

The dining room is large, with an oval mahogany table in the center of the room. There are over a dozen seats at the table. Next to each seat is a plush pillow with a dark red damask pattern on it. The dark red and gold accents give the room a warm and rich feeling.

Although the room is large with many chairs, there are only three people in the room. Gabriel, with Talia by his side, and another man I don't know at the chairs.

"You've finally decided to join us?" Gabriel asks Kade as we walk through the stained-glass double doors. Gabriel's at the head of the table and farthest away from us. Talia's seated on the pillow beside him. I can only see a bit of her hair until we walk farther into the room and Kade takes a seat next to Gabriel. I kneel onto the pillow beside him. My heart hammers in my chest.

"I think she's ready for a bit of socializing."

Kade's hand settles on my shoulder, his thumb rubbing soothing circles. I finally look over at Talia, and she seems perfectly content. Her hand rests on Gabriel's thigh, and his hand is on top of hers.

Her eyes meet mine and she gives me a soft smile. She closes her eyes and when she opens them, she's no longer looking at me. "It's about time," I hear Gabriel say. "More guests are coming tomorrow. It should be fun."

"Stone?" Kade asks.

Gabriel shakes his head. "He called again though." Irritation laces Gabriel's voice. "He's an impatient asshole, isn't he?"

I watch a woman walk into the room and hear her set something down on the table. Because I'm seated on the floor, I can only see her lower half. "Who's an asshole now?" says a voice I recognize, and turn to my left. Master A walks across the room and sits to the left of Kade, directly next to me.

"No company tonight, Master A?" Gabriel asks.

"There's plenty of company in here," Master A says. I quickly turn to face the ground as he looks at me with a smile.

"Isn't that right, Olivia?" Master A asks me.

I look up as my heart races. I swallow thickly and try to respond. My body heats with anxiety.

"It's alright, angel." Kade's calming voice puts me a bit at ease.

"She's scared, Master," Talia says, looking up at Gabriel.

I look between the men as I try to breathe normally. They're all looking at me, and I don't know what to do. I weakly respond with a "Yes, sir."

"Come up here, *esclave*." Gabriel puts a hand down for

Talia and she easily slides into his lap, molding her body to his and letting her legs dangle over his.

Kade reaches his hand down. "You, too."

I do the same as Talia, mimicking her pose and look to her for clues on what I'm supposed to be doing. Her eyes are fixed on the large bowls and platters in the center of the table. The smell of butter and salmon fills my lungs. My mouth waters as I see the crusted fish on a silver tray with bowls of asparagus and potatoes next to it. Salmon is one of my favorite meals and the fillets look perfect, as though they came straight from a picture in a recipe book. The man across the table uses the tongs to dish some greens onto his plate.

Gabriel puts a fillet on his own plate and passes the utensil to Kade.

I lick my lips at the sight of the fillet. I want to reach out and dig in, but I don't. I resist. I watch as Talia picks up a fork and starts eating. Gabriel pets her hair and continues a conversation with the man across the table. I keep my hands in my lap, knowing I shouldn't do anything until Kade allows me.

Every meal I've had here so far he's fed me. I peek at Talia as she picks up a piece of asparagus with her fingers and nibbles delicately on the tip. She leans back against Gabriel and watches him and the other man as they talk.

"I didn't mean to make you uncomfortable." I hear

Master A's voice and I turn to him and try to respond. I don't know what to say though. I'm at a complete loss. I know how to do what I'm told, but I don't know how to talk to anyone or what I can do if I'm not given direction.

Other than to call them sir, since I sure as fuck remember that. I need to know the rules for socializing, but I don't. I feel lost.

"Well I know she's keeping you busy, Master K, but do you even talk to the poor woman?" Gabriel asks with humor. Kade lets out a humorless laugh. My breath stills in my lungs, and tears prick my eyes. I'm supposed to be perfect for him. I'm failing.

Talia reaches across the table and takes my hand in hers. She wipes her other hand on the napkin. Her eyes are full of remorse. "It can be hard at first, but you're doing so well, I mean it." She gives me a smile, and part of me wants to hate her for condoning the way I'm being treated; the other half wants to hug her for her kindness.

I swallow thickly and give her a tight smile. "Thank you."

"She'll learn," Kade responds simply. He leans forward and my body is pushed against the table as he grabs a bottle of wine. "This will help." As he leans back, he wraps his arm around my waist and pulls me closer to him. He pours a large glass of wine and moves it closer to me. He kisses my hair, and when I look up at him he seems happy.

He's not upset with me, which is a relief.

He jostles my body as he leans back, and I have to put my hands out and brace myself against his chest to steady myself.

"Honestly, I'm sure she's ready," Master A says. *Ready for what?*

"I'm not." Kade answers quickly before Gabriel can respond. "I want her to be perfect."

My body chills at his words. I don't know what they're referring to, but I've done everything he's asked.

"I'm trying," I barely manage to say. Kade looks down at me, and his face softens. "You're doing perfectly, angel." His praise makes my tense body relax. "You just need a little time."

"I have to say I'm impressed, Master K," the man I don't know says from across the table. "My pet took much longer to come around."

"Where is she now, Master W?" Gabriel asks him with his eyebrows raised.

"In bed," Master W replies with a smirk. "She had a long day."

The men all chuckle, and Talia lets a smile play at her lips, as if she's in on some joke.

"We do enjoy the training lessons, but they exhaust her."

Master A takes a napkin off the table and smooths it

over his lap before reaching for the bottle of wine. "Master W and his wife started coming here a few years ago." He lowers his voice and leans in closer to me as he says, "Their situation is a little different from yours."

My body tenses, and I look back at Master W with adrenaline racing through me. Kade stiffens and holds me a bit tighter.

Master W and his *wife*. My heart pounds with the need to escape. Wife, not slave. My eyes dart from the table to the man, and my hands grips onto my thighs as though they'll fly away if I let go.

Maybe he doesn't know. Maybe he could help me.

I want to scream and tell Master W I need his help. I want to plead with him to call the cops. I remember the party and how I wondered if the women were there willingly or not. Am I the only one here by force? How stupid have I been not to try to run?

My chest tightens with pain as I think about the days I've spent wanting to be free, but too scared to run. Maybe I could've escaped already. My body turns to ice as I open my mouth.

My throat dries as I look back at Master W. His eyes are fixed on his plate as he picks up his fork. Kade lowers his lips to my ear and grips on to me tighter as he says, "Think very hard about what you're going to say, angel." My body freezes with fear.

I feel a pang of guilt and I'm nearly overwhelmed with anxiety. I feel like I'm betraying Kade, I know that..

I swallow thickly and prepare to scream for help. I have to try. I have to. My heart clenches in my chest. I have to at least try. I'm acutely aware in this moment that I feel something for Kade, but I'm not his property. I need to get the fuck out of here.

"Help me!" I barely get the words out as they rip from my throat. Kade's hand closes over my mouth tightly, and he forces my head back so I'm staring at the ceiling.

The legs of Kade's chair squeak against the wooden floor as he pushes us away from the table. His legs wrap around mine as I kick out and hit the hard table. It hurts, but I barely register the pain. Kade's arm wraps around mine and effectively holds me completely still. My heart races, and my body is a mix of hot and cold, a sickness threatening to lose itself.

"Whoa!" Master A yells out, and stands up from the table. I see his wine spill across the dark wood and onto the floor. "No worries," he says, putting his napkin on the table.

My heart stills, no one's reacted at all to my cry for help. My chest feels hollow as I see the man across the table looking at me with pity as he picks up his glass of water.

Useless. It was for nothing.

Tears leak down my cheeks. *Help me.* My heart lurches in my chest.

"You were right," I hear Gabriel say. "She's not quite

ready, but still, she's doing wonderfully considering how new she is." He's speaking casually, as though I didn't just scream for help. As though Kade's not holding me still because I was flailing my body and screaming.

My body goes limp in Kade's arms. There's no use fighting.

"Are you done?" Kade asks with a low, threatening voice. My eyes squeeze shut. No, no. I wish I could take it back.

I try to nod my head, but his hand over my mouth is so forceful that I can't move my head. He slowly drops it to my throat and I'm quick to answer, "Yes, Master."

I feel defeated, betrayed, alone, and ashamed. My breath is unsteady as I try to calm myself. The three other men continue to eat as though nothing's happened, and everything is alright.

Talia looks at me with sympathy in her blue eyes. She sets her fork down and leans against Gabriel, refusing to meet my gaze. Her plump lips are turned down and it makes me feel so alone.

No one here is going to help me. Even worse, I feel guilty.

"Well that was bound to happen," Gabriel says in a casual voice as though he's trying to lighten the mood.

Kade's tight hold on me loosens, and I see the man across the table nodding while chewing whatever he just put in his mouth.

My body's stiff as Kade sets me back down in his lap. Everyone else has resumed to normal, although Talia's not eating. I watch as Gabriel picks up a piece of asparagus and puts it to her lips, but she shakes her head and leans against him, burying her head under his chin.

I stare at her and will her to look at me, but she does nothing. I feel sick to my stomach.

"What are you thinking, Master K?" Gabriel asks. He takes a bite of the asparagus and chews it as he waits for Kade to answer. I lower my eyes to the floor. Fuck. I try to breathe in and out slowly, but even doing that is hard.

"It's her first offense since we've been here." Kade's voice sends a chill up my back.

"But it was a grave offense." I watch as Talia shifts in Gabriel's lap, uneasy with the topic of conversation.

I can feel Kade nodding behind me. "I'll finish my dinner first."

"And then what?" Master A asks.

Kade picks up the tongs and dishes out a few spears of asparagus onto the plate. His movements jostle my body, but I try to stay upright. They're talking about me as if I'm not in the room. Talking about my punishment. I close my eyes and wish I'd never done it.

I had to though.

My body freezes at Kade's response. "When I'm done eating, we'll go to the basement."

CHAPTER 19

Olivia

I WALK BEHIND KADE OBEDIENTLY, EVEN THOUGH he's leading me to my punishment. I can hardly breathe, my chest hurts so much.

Kade stops at a door to the right of the stairs. His hand rests on the knob as he turns to me. "I understand why you did that, Olivia. I do. But you know it was bad, don't you?"

My stomach churns as I nod my head and answer, "Yes, Master K."

No, no it wasn't. I *had* to. He grips my chin in his hand and forces me to look into his narrowed eyes. He looks pissed. My heart stops in my chest.

"Don't lie to me, angel." His words are hard and unforgiving. "I'm thankful it happened in that company. Had it been different..." he trails off as he opens the door and takes in a slow inhale. He doesn't finish what he was saying, leaving me to imagine the worst, but instead walks down the steps.

I take a peek into the basement. It's different down here. It's not luxurious at all. The walls are cinderblocks that have been painted grey. The steps are wooden and also painted, although they're black and have texture to them. My heart races as Kade descends the stairs. I look to my right and I know the front doors are close. They're just down the hall. I could try to run. A very large part of me wants to.

I take an uneasy step toward the basement door and grip the handle. I could close the door and try to run.

My heart races and thuds in my chest.

"Don't make me wait for you, angel." Although Kade's voice is low and laced with a threat, it eases something inside of me. I let go of the door and walk slowly down the wooden stairs. When I look to my left I can see the room for what it is. It's mostly empty. The floor is painted black, and the walls are the same grey-painted cinders. There's a drain in the center of the room, and nothing else. It's empty.

My heart slows as I think of what this room could be used for. I nearly trip on the last stair as my heart tries to leap out of my throat.

Murder, death. The drain is for blood. That must be it. My hand grips the railing, but my feet are bolted to the ground.

"Olivia, calm down. It's okay." Kade puts his hands up and his eyes soften. "It's alright, angel." His voice is meant to calm me, but it's not working. He walks to me with even steps, and it takes everything in me not to move away from him. "I'm not going to hurt you." He sounds so sincere. I lift my eyes to meet his, and he slowly drops his lips to mine. His hand cups the back of my head.

His comforting touch feels so welcoming. I lean into him and deepen the kiss. I'll be good. I can be good. My heart swells in my chest. I want to make this right.

He pulls away from me and wraps his hand lightly around my throat. "Olivia," he begins and pauses to take in a deep breath. "You weren't supposed to do that." Sadness clouds his eyes.

"I'm sorry." I really feel like I betrayed him. I remember what he said, and his promise to free me. I'm so fucking stupid. I take in a ragged breath.

"Please, Kade," I say and place my hand on his hard chest as I beg him. "I won't do it again. I promise."

"Angel, I wish it were that easy." He takes my hand in

both of his and leads me across the room. Under the stairs is a bench covered in a wipeable material and on either side of it are two storage containers.

"I want you to lie down on the bench." Kade doesn't even look at me as he gives me his order. I walk slowly to the bench and lie down on my back. The bench is wide enough to easily fit me, and long enough so that there's plenty of seating left over.

My heart races as Kade opens a box and then the other. I want to look at what he's getting, but I don't. I'm terrified. I close my eyes tight and clench my fists.

Just obey, and soon I'll be free. I can do this.

My eyes pop open as I hear chains above my head. I look up, and sure enough, two chains with shackles are now dangling from the stairs. Kade adjusts them so he can easily lock the shackles around my ankles, then he raises and spreads them wide. Each side of the staircase has a chain affixed. The thin dress I'm wearing slides up, and the cool air breathes against my bared pussy. I swallow thickly, knowing I'm completely vulnerable like this.

"Kade," I breathe out.

"Yes, Olivia?"

"What are you going to do to me?" I ask. I need to know.

"I'm going to deny you, angel."

"Deny me what?" I ask as he places a thick strip of cloth

over my torso before wrapping and locking a chain around it. Now I'm chained to the bench with my legs in the air, completely spread wide open for him.

He gives me a soft smile and pushes the hair out of my face, but he doesn't answer me.

"You don't have to chain me," I say as he reaches into one of the boxes. He looks at me with a cocked brow. "The chain around my stomach," I say and clear my dry throat. "I promise I won't move." I won't. I'm going to be good for him.

He smirks at me and shakes his head. "You won't intend to move, but you will. That chain is for your safety. I don't want you to fall." He closes the box and looks to the stairs as he takes something out of his pocket. My eyes widen. It's the egg from earlier.

I breathe out as he slips the egg into place. He has to pump it in and out before it's fully in place. I'm not at all aroused.

"I'm not used to you not being wet for me," Kade remarks as he reaches back into his pocket and grabs the controller. "You must really dislike being punished."

No shit. Nothing like thinking you're going to die to turn you off.

I hold onto my snarky remark and try to forget everything. *Just obey.* I can do this.

Kade flips the switch and a gentle hum fills the room.

It doesn't feel the same as earlier. It's on a low speed, and I'm not anywhere near on edge.

My fingers twitch at my sides, and Kade sees. He's quick to cuff my wrists to the chain around my stomach.

"Are you comfortable?" Kade asks. The shackles on my ankle bite a bit into my skin, but other than that I am, yeah. I nod my head and search Kade's eyes for answers.

The humming seems to get louder and the vibrations more intense. It's just enough that my pussy heats, and desire spikes, but then it's gone. I try to readjust, feeling off-balance, but I can't. I can't move anything. "I have to blindfold you now," Kade says, and I shake my head out of instinct. I don't want that. Not being able to see terrifies me.

"You don't have a say in this, angel," Kade says as he slips a black blindfold over my eyes. I hold in a moan as the vibrations increase again and my forehead scrunches. I try to twist my hips, but I'm limited, and it only makes my ankles hurt from putting pressure on them.

In an instant, the sensation is gone again and I feel on edge. I can tell there's light, but other than that, I'm blind.

"Kade," I whisper. There's no response. "Kade?" I call for him with desperation.

"I'm here, angel." I wish he'd hold me.

I scream out as the vibrations pick up again and I try to

buck my hips to get away, but I can't. My body heats as I get closer to my heightened orgasm, but then it dies.

My heart races, and my pussy clenches.

I breathe out slowly.

I swallow and attempt to ignore it. I try to ignore the arousal pooling in my core, the heated tingles along my stomach and legs. My nipples have hardened, and every small movement against the dress seems to elicit a shock of electricity straight to my clit.

The vibrations intensify again, and this time I try to rock my hips. I just need a bit more. It's so close, yet so far away. I whimper a small moan as they die down, leaving me feeling needy and helpless.

When it doesn't come, I lie limp and try to remember to breathe.

And then again, and again.

I clench my teeth as each time my orgasm approaches, I almost fear the moment I fall off the edge. My toes and extremities tingle with need. My body feels as though it's going to explode, each time greater than the last... yet nothing happens.

My arousal drips down my ass and onto the seat. I want to move. I pull against the chains, but I can't do anything. I'm forced to scream out as the next one comes and goes. Leaving my body to fight against both the upcoming release, and the inevitable denial of it.

"Kade!" I cry out for him. But I hear nothing. "I'm sorry!" I scream as it comes again.

I buck my hips and try desperately to find my release.

My body heats and cools as a thin sheen of sweat covers every inch.

And then nothing.

My head thrashes, and my heart beats up my throat as I try to both fight and conquer the heated sensation.

The faint hum of the vibrator is the only noise in the room.

And it's the only sound other than my own moans and screams for god knows how long.

It feels like hours.

Tears leak down my face as it comes again, with the relentless sensation, but this time there's more. A strangled cry leaves my mouth as I get closer than I ever have before.

Relief blooms in my chest. The intensity picks up and just as I begin to fall, the vibrations stop completely.

I scream out in both anger and frustration. I feel delirious.

The room is quiet other than my frantic breathing. Even the hum I've listened to the entire time has left me.

I try to calm down, thinking maybe it's over. My punishment is finally done with. But then the faint hum comes back with the soft vibrations, and I lose all sense of composure.

I scream out for Kade until my throat hurts. Sweat covers my heated body and I pull against the chains and thrash on the bench as my punishment seems to last and last.

I don't know how long it's been. But each time it hurts more and more to be teased and denied.

I focus on trying to accept it won't come. This is my punishment.

I'm only distracted by the small sounds of footprints coming down the stairs.

"Kade?" I call out for him in a choked voice. "Please!"

"Shh!" a soft feminine voice says as the egg is pulled away from me.

Relief. Oh, fuck! Thank fuck.

I turn my head to the side as my body goes limp although my legs are still trembling.

The blindfold is pulled away, and I wince from the light.

"Talia?" I blink several times until she comes into focus. "Please let me out," I whisper harshly.

"I can't. Please. I just came for a moment." A sob is ripped up my throat.

"I can't stay here," I whimper.

"It's okay," she says sweetly, wiping the tears from my face. "He just left, so I thought I'd sneak in."

I don't understand what she's saying. "Who?"

"I'm sure he'll be right back, and hopefully he'll end it soon."

"Kade?" I ask her, my body tense.

She nods her head and wipes my face with a cool cloth. It feels so good. So good. I feel so hot. "The first time is the worst." I don't know if she's talking to me or to herself.

"Please!" I scream out, and she covers my mouth with her hand.

"Shh! I'll get in so much trouble for coming down here if I'm caught." The nervousness in her voice makes me try to calm my breathing and listen for any new sounds, but there's nothing.

She slowly lifts her hand away from my mouth and I beg her, "Please, please let me out."

"I can't. I'm so sorry, Olivia."

"You don't know what it's like," I say and take in a ragged breath. "I don't want this like you do."

She scoffs at me and it catches me off-guard. "I know exactly what it's like." There's a moment of silence as she looks up the stairs. My body is begging to move. I'm still so close. I try to ignore it, but part of me shamelessly wants me to beg her to get me off. I bite down on my lip and ignore the intense need claiming my every thought.

"It was much worse for me, trust me. It wasn't always this way." Her voice sounds lost. "It's really not so bad, is it?" she asks.

I can't answer. I turn my head to look away. Partly

because of her question, and partly because of my debilitating needs.

After a moment, she starts talking again. "Master A feels really bad. He didn't think you'd do that."

"Did he tell you that?" I ask weakly. My body calms slightly as the absence of stimulation lengthens. I turn back to look at her; I'm grateful for the distraction.

She shakes her head and looks back up at the stairs. "He was talking to Master G."

"They were talking about me?" I ask weakly, still partially out of breath. Fuck, that can't be good.

She lets out a small giggle at my worried look and explains, "They were hoping your master would let them help."

"They want to punish me?" My heart lurches in my chest. My body is still on edge and I'm trying to ignore it. The fear of her confession helps.

"No, no, afterward. They thought he would spank and then fuck you at the table."

My pussy clenches at her words, and the small movement makes my clit throb. I throw my head back and moan. I can see him doing it. Fuck, it's so wrong, but the thought turns me on. I wish he'd just done that. My back arches as I think about what she said. *How they wanted to help.* And then I realize it's her Master and he said that to her.

"He'd do that to you?" I feel so bad for her.

She arches a brow. "Spank and fuck me? Of course," she says and practically rolls her eyes.

"No, fuck... fuck someone else in front of you." It feels weird talking to her about this. But they seem like a couple. I can't imagine how much it must hurt her.

She gives me a soft smile. "He would." She leans in and adds, "I like to help, too."

I can feel shock the moment the meaning of her words hits me. My mouth pops open slightly, and I don't know how to respond. I try to speak, but I don't know what to say.

"It's okay, I'm not sad that you don't want to fuck me. I prefer the dicks, too." She winks at me, but I'm stiff and unsure of how to respond at all.

"I have to go; he'll be back soon," she says hastily, as if this conversation wasn't uncomfortable.

If I could I'd grip her arm to keep her from leaving, I would, but I can't.

I see her reach down the bench as the humming comes back to life.

"No!" Fuck, no! I can't. I can't take this any longer.

"Please don't ask me to do something I can't." Her forehead is creased, and her clear blue eyes are so sad. "It's going to be okay, Olivia. He'll make sure you're taken care of. I promise you."

She quickly places the blindfold back over my eyes and I pathetically begin to cry.

"It's okay, it's going to be okay," she reassures me.

"But it's not," I manage to choke out. She slowly puts the egg that's still vibrating back into place, and I start crying again. I can't take it. I can't help it.

"I'm so sorry." I can hear the sorrow in her voice. "Please, don't worry. It'll be okay."

I listen as she leaves, and try to rein in my pathetic sobs. She quickly climbs up the stairs and gently closes the door.

As I strain against the cuffs feeling a wave of arousal come I know will only heighten and torture me over time, I swear I hear the faint sound of the door opening.

I listen as hard as I can, but I don't hear his steps. I hold my breath. Finally, I hear a creak on the stairs and then the next, and then nothing.

"Kade," I call out. "Please—" My words are cut short as I struggle against the intense vibrations yet again. My body heats, and my back bows. So close. So close. Please.

And then nothing.

"Shh, angel."

"Kade," I say and turn toward him as best I can, which isn't much. "Please," I beg.

He doesn't answer me, but in an instant the egg is removed and in its place are his fingers. He pumps them in and out of my slick heat and pushes his thumb against my clit. It doesn't take long until I'm close to the overwhelming edge of my impending release. My body heats with a vengeance, and every nerve ending quickly goes numb before exploding with pleasure. My mouth falls open, and my body shudders as wave after wave courses through my body. A white light flashes before my eyes as he pulls my orgasm from me. In an instant it's over and I quickly crash, feeling drained and numb.

My body falls limp, feeling nearly paralyzed. He unchains one leg and then the other, and they fall heavily into his arms. He lowers them to the bench, and I feel the wetness on the back of my legs.

It takes a long time before I register what's happening. My eyes are heavy, and so is my body.

I groan as he massages life back into my legs.

"Kade," I whisper in a soft voice.

He removes the cuffs and then the chain around my stomach. And again he massages my arms and shoulders.

I cry silently with relief as he lifts me into his arms and wraps a blanket around me. Finally, he slowly removes the blindfold and I bury my head into his chest.

"Shh, it's alright, angel. It's over."

He whispers into my hair and kisses my forehead as he carries me to the bedroom.

The last thing I remember before I pass out is him laying me gently on the bed and pulling my back against his chest.

He plants a small kiss on my neck. "It's alright, angel. I've got you."

CHAPTER 20

Kade

LAST NIGHT WAS TOO MUCH. I DON'T KNOW WHY, but I couldn't get James out of my head. I fucking killed him. I shot him in cold blood, for fuck's sake. I should be more focused on the case. I should be more invested. But something about this house, something about *her*, is keeping me from wanting this to end.

It's wrong. It's fucked up. But somehow my focus has switched. I close my eyes and try to calm myself. This had to happen. I *have* to play the part. And I am. I'm playing it damn well.

After I left her asleep last night, I went back downstairs. I thought I handled it well, and I was right. They're impressed more than anything else. Even Olivia is playing the part perfectly. She doesn't even know it.

She's doing so well, I think as the hot water from the shower flows down my body. She's so fucking perfect. They saw her fear and anxiety and how she obeyed me regardless. And now she's the perfect example of obedience. Well, other than her little outburst. I hope she got that shit out of her system.

I knew it would happen. I don't blame her in the least. That's why I chose last night to test her when I knew it would only be a few people. Close friends. Except for William. I could have done without him being there.

I know she's on edge. She's feeling trapped and uneasy. She's practically walking on eggshells every time I bring her outside the bedroom. She doesn't trust anyone else, but she sure as fuck trusts me. She just needs to let go and realize she doesn't have to think about it so hard.

I'll take care of her. All she needs to do is trust me. And she's so close.

My heart pumps faster in my chest and my dick twitches as the water runs down my body. Punishing her was harder than I thought. I wanted to do so much more than deprive her. Every moan and twist of her body made me want to pound her tight pussy. But I haven't taken it that far yet. I need to. They need to see it. It's much harder to resist her when she's fully submitting to me. And she did that last night. Fuck, just the memory of it has my dick at full attention.

I open my eyes as I hear the door creak open and a breeze disturb the comforting heat around me. It closes quickly, and her bare feet patter against the floor.

"Angel?" My brows raise as I see her slowly walk toward the shower. I move the glass door open and watch as she lowers herself into the tiled floor. She's completely naked. I took off her clothes last night and her collar. Everything needed to be cleaned after her punishment.

She looks so fragile and delicate.

My heart slows in my chest. This is new. It must have taken a lot for her to approach me. She's learning that she doesn't need to wait in order to things that would please me. That's a good sign. I wait for her to speak.

"Kade, I—" She clears her throat before looking up at me with wide eyes. "I'm sorry."

"You're sorry you were punished." I keep my voice even and hard. I could see it in her eyes before I took her downstairs. She wasn't sorry she tried to get away. She was sorry it didn't work. I'm not sure she'd do it again though. I'm not positive either way, and that's a problem.

She shakes her head. "I'm sorry," she barely speaks; her voice is choked. Her small whimper breaks my heart. The need to ease her worries is strong. She needs me, almost as much as I need her.

"It's over now, angel."

"Can I—" her voice cuts off as her eyes dart to the ground then back up to mine. "Can I come in with you?" she asks with a small voice. She looks nervous and vulnerable.

This is the first time she's initiated any interaction with me. I need to make sure I reward this behavior. She needs the comfort, too. She needs to know I'm not angry with her, and that she's completely forgiven. And she is. There's nothing that truly needs to be forgiven. I don't want her to worry. That would be detrimental for both of us.

I answer her question with a simple nod. "Come."

She rises slowly and I open the door wider so she can walk in. She stands in the steam a moment. The hot water splashes against her feet as she hesitantly holds her hand out, testing the temperature. Without her body full immersed, her nipples begin to harden. She takes a small step forward, and her milky white skin turns pink with a beautiful flush from the heat.

My dick immediately starts hardening.

Her small hands rest at my hips, and she leans into me resting her head on my chest. I turn her slightly so the water runs along her back and into her hair.

I reach for the soap, and she turns to watch. "Can I wash you?" she asks.

She's in such need, my poor, sweet angel. "You can."

She eagerly pours a bit of soap into her hands and rubs them together to make a frothy bit of suds. I watch her face intently. She seems so serious, like she needs to do this perfectly. She's scared still. I want to ease that fear. I place my hand on her lower back and pull her body close to mine.

My hard cock presses against her lower belly. She looks up through her thick lashes, with her plump lips parted and I give in.

I can't resist giving us what we both need.

I lower my lips to hers and push her back against the tiled wall.

Her back bows, and she pushes her breasts against my chest. Her mouth parts for me and she moans into my mouth. Her hands grip onto my shoulders, pulling me closer to her.

I grip her thighs in my hands and lift her up. She wraps her legs around my waist and digs her heels into my ass. With one hand on her ass and the other in her hair, I pull away from her and look down at her. She's panting with half-lidded eyes.

There's nothing but lust in her gorgeous eyes.

She wants me.

I leave open-mouthed kisses on her neck and rock my hard dick against her clit.

"Uh!" She lets out a strangled cry as I nip her neck. Her blunt fingernails dig into my shoulders. "Kade," she whimpers. I kiss and suck and bit along her neck and up her jaw. I angle my hips so she's steady against the wall, and move my hand to her breast.

I kiss her soft and gently as her breathing calms.

She fits perfectly in my hand. I roll her hardened peaks between my fingers and pinch.

"Ah!" she exclaims as she throws her head back, and I feel her pussy clench down on the side of my dick, nestled between her lips.

"Tell me you want me, angel," I whisper into her ear. The sounds of the water splashing is loud, but she hears me.

Her hand settles on my jaw and she looks deep into my eyes. "I want you," she breathes out quickly.

In one swift move, I push all of myself deep inside of her. Her body slams hard against the tile and her head falls forward, her forehead pressed to mine. Her mouth opens into a perfect O as she holds in a scream of pleasure.

I stay deep inside of her tight cunt as her pussy spasms around my dick.

A low rough groan is forced from my throat. She feels so fucking good. So hot and tight.

I give her a moment to adjust to my size and push my lips against hers. Her forehead is still pinched and her lips are hard at first, but she softens them. Her breathing picks up as I thrust my hips, pulling almost all the way out and then pushing all the way back in. I slide as deep as I can each time.

I force soft moans out of those plump lips with every pump. I fucking love the sounds she's making.

I dip my tongue into her mouth and she eagerly kisses me back. I deepen the kiss as I pick up my pace, fucking her ruthlessly against the cold, hard wall. Yes! I struggle to stay in control. I've wanted her for so long.

Her moans and the sounds of the water streaming in the shower are the only things I can hear as I buck my hips against hers over and over. My spine tingles and my balls draw up, but I need her to cum with me.

I angle my hips so I'm pushing against her clit and thrust shallow pumps into her heat. She bites down on her lip and throws her head to the side. I fucking love the sight of her so vulnerable. So close to pleasure, yet it's a dangerous edge, letting go and allowing it to overpower her. She knows she'll be shattered, and she's fighting it. She has the urge to race to the end and be overwhelmed with the sensation of cumming with me, but also the desire to prevent it from happening altogether.

"Please," she pushes the word out, and I cave into her desires.

I push harder and faster, and make sure each thrust hits her throbbing clit. I slam my dick into her all the way to the hilt and still deep inside of her as jets of hot cum leave me in waves. My spine tingles, and waves of pleasure flow through my body. I feel her body stiffen and her walls tighten, then the most beautiful sounds I've ever heard spill from her lips. Her head pushes against the wall as she cums violently. Her eyes are closed and I stare at her face, loving how fucking beautiful she is like this.

If I could keep this moment forever, I would. But this moment doesn't belong to us. I gently kiss her full lips as the high of our lust dims.

I wish things were different. I wish she really was mine to keep. But she's not.

I wish I could keep her forever, but I can't.

My eyes slowly open and I stare at her gorgeous face. Her eyes are closed in complete rapture. I can try to keep her though. I have to try. I don't want to let her go.

CHAPTER 21

Olivia

"YOU NEED TO GET READY FOR TONIGHT," KADE
says as I brush my hair. I set it down on the vanity. It's filled
with new makeup and expensive perfumes and lotions I'd
never dreamed of having. There are clothes in the closet
too, although I've barely worn any of them.

Kade prefers me in the same handful of dresses when
we're outside of the bedroom. But he said we'll be leaving
soon. And I'll need them once we leave here.

I haven't forgotten what this place is. It's a gilded cage. Although it is a comfortable one.

The thought of getting away from here brings back my desire to run full force. I keep the thoughts at bay as best I can so I don't slip up. I need to be perfect and leave this place unscathed. I'm so close, just days away now until he takes me back. I know his guard is down, and I may be given the chance to take my own freedom, rather than waiting for him to gift it to me.

"You look beautiful, angel." His soft praise interrupts my thoughts, and I look up into his blue eyes as he grips the top of the chair behind me. My heart swells. I don't know how fucked up I am, but there's something wrong with me. I crave his approval. And I love it when he gives it to me.

❖ ❖ ❖

I kneel on the floor next to Kade. There are several chairs in the large room, although most people are standing closer to the stage. We're on the side wall with an unhindered view. To my right is Kade, his hand on my shoulder, rubbing soothing circles as I sit perfectly still in the kneeling position. Gabriel is on my left, and next to him is Talia.

I keep wanting to look at her, but I don't. I haven't had a moment to talk to her since... my punishment. I want to thank her; I haven't had a chance to though.

In the center of the stage is a slave and her Master. I'm

not certain if she's like me and Talia, or like Master W's wife. I know not to ask.

She's shackled to a post in the center of the stage. Her Master's fingering her and she's pulling against the chains. His corded muscles ripple as he shoves his fingers into her soaked pussy. He pumps them in and out and kisses her neck, biting and moving up her jaw. Her back tries to bow, and she screams out sounds of pleasure.

The dim lights are centered on them, and the rest of the room is practically pitch black. But I can see the audience just fine. My eyes have adjusted to the darkness. Some couples watch as the Master covers her eyes with a sash and pulls a toy from his pocket. Other couples engage in their own activities. The man on stage commands her to open her mouth, and she does so eagerly. She sucks on the plug, warming it and getting it wet before he inserts it into her ass. She squirms slightly as he works it in and out.

That's one thing Kade hasn't done with me. Of all the things he's done, he's never done anything other than spank my ass. He said he wants my pussy. And I'm his alone, so there's no need for me to be trained otherwise.

The woman screams out as he smacks her clit with a riding crop, spreading her pussy lips and doing it over and over. His movements are harsh, although the crop is barely touching her with light flicks. But I imagine the sensation of not knowing when they're coming is nearly too much to bear. I know when he's done with her she'll be limp and sated. But that could take hours, and there's no telling what all will happen between now and then.

"When will Olivia be ready for us?" I don't react to Gabriel's question. I anticipated this.

It's like a fucking graduation ceremony. Although I'm nervous and feeling a little uneasy about the idea of everyone watching, I trust Kade. He's not going to let anything happen to me. He'll keep me safe and take me away once all this is done. And a darker part of me is looking forward to it. When he trains me now, it's just like this. My core heats as I think about yesterday.

He didn't have to tie me up. I'm much better now at resisting the urge to move away. He made me wait to cum. He brought me to the edge, and I was able to hold it there. I waited until he said I could. It's much easier to do when he's simply hitting my clit like the Master's doing on stage. I can go for a long time without cumming then. But the vibrator or Kade fucking me is much more difficult. Both are just so intense. Too intense to control.

It took days of practice to get to this point. He said it was his fault though that it took so long for me to learn. Every time I came without his consent he fucked me mercilessly. But that's not a punishment. Not that he's ever punished me beyond the one time. As long as I'm trying, and as long as I submit to him, then I don't deserve any negative consequences.

"I think she's ready for us right now," Master A says as he walks closer to us. I hadn't seen him in the room. My eyes widen slightly when I see the look in his eyes.

My pussy clenches as I realize the double meaning of their words.

A soft rumble comes from Kade's chest as I close my eyes and look at the ground.

"Are you ready for me, Olivia?" Master A asks.

My breath stills in my lungs as I peek up at him.

"I'm ready when Master K tells me I am, sir." I keep my voice low and my face neutral, but the thought of being commanded by Kade on the stage only makes me even more turned on. I try not to show it, but judging from Gabriel's chuckle, I've failed.

For some reason, knowing this is all going to end soon, and feeling so safe with Kade, I almost want to answer differently. I almost call him Master, but I don't.

Master A pouts comically and leans against the wall to Kade's right.

"Well, you can't blame a man for trying."

I lean against Kade's leg and he runs his hand through my hair, petting me.

As the night continues, I consider just how completely

broken I am. The sight on the stage doesn't affect me in any way other than to arouse me. *I want to be her.* At what point did I come to trust a man who's dangerous and took me as a sex slave? When did I start desiring being used? But most importantly, why am I not in a hurry to leave?

CHAPTER 22

Olivia

I TAKE KADE'S HAND AS I STEP OUT OF THE shower. The hot steam with the scent of lavender fills my lungs as I step onto the cold tile floor. It's so relaxing.

Every night he's done this for I don't even know how many days now. It's always the same routine. He feeds me, trains me, bathes me, and then takes me downstairs. He says dinner and the show are for training. But I don't do anything. I don't understand. It's simple, I obey him.

Always. He's never pushed me to do anything other than stay beside him.

When we get back to the bedroom, the atmosphere changes. I get lost in his touch. The heat in his eyes is so intense that I feel alive and vibrant. He commands me, but not in any way that seems unnatural to our relationship. Nothing that makes me want to say no. I want everything he gives me. And he gives me everything I want. I fall asleep feeling safe and warm beside him.

But it's the same thing every day. Nothing has changed.

He never leaves my side, which I both love and hate. I need the security; this house itself still scares me. Sometimes I feel like Kade's my bodyguard, and other times he's my warden.

"Why do you always come in with me? I'm not going to do anything stupid." I don't know if that's completely true though. Even knowing my freedom is close, I've thought about doing something stupid a time or two. But I'd never do it.

The idea that he's going to let me walk away does strange things to me. I push down the emotions threatening to creep up on me and ignore it. It's still days away. Possibly more before we leave here, and then who knows if I'll be able to escape. If not, I'll have to wait.

The idea of waiting doesn't make me tense or anxious. It's a different emotion, one I'm not comfortable exploring.

I should want to leave, and I do. But the thought still makes me upset. I want to leave, but I want to bring Kade with me. It doesn't make sense.

Kade chuckles low and deep. Being in the small confines of the bathroom makes it sound even sexier somehow.

"Because I like touching you." My nipples pebble as I lift my arms for him to wrap a towel around me.

"Tonight," Kade starts but stops as his forehead pinches. "Tonight you're going to be on the stage, angel." He doesn't look at me as he takes a deep breath.

"What do you think about that?" he asks. I'm surprised he's asking me my opinion.

"If you think I'm ready, then I'll be perfect for you. I'll do the best I can." I search his face and will him to look at me, and he does.

But there's a hint of fear there I've never seen before.

"You're different from the others, angel." Kade sits on the windowsill and pulls me between his legs. "I never should have offered you freedom."

My heart stills in my chest, and I almost take a step backward.

"No, no, it's yours. I would have given it to you regardless." He lowers his nose to mine with his eyes closed. "I made you that promise, and I meant it."

"I don't understand." Why is he saying that?

He stares into my eyes. "You didn't fight me. Only that once."

"Isn't that a good thing?"

He takes a deep breath. "They're going to want me to push you, they're going to want to see that I'm taking you to your limits."

"Do you trust me?" Kade asks.

I nod my head. I do trust him. I don't know why, and I know I probably shouldn't, but I do.

"If I ever put you in a situation you don't want to be in, I want you to give me a sign, angel."

My heart's beating faster and I start questioning if I can do this. "What are you going to do?"

"I can't tell you, angel. It's not for me to decide." What? I don't like that.

"Gabriel gets to pick what's done on the stage."

My breathing stills, and my pussy clenches.

Kade arches a brow at me. He grips my hips in both his hands and pulls me close to him. He whispers in the crook of my neck, "That doesn't upset you, does it?"

I know what he's really asking, and I'm quick to answer, "I'm yours, and only yours."

"There's no doubt in my mind that's true."

I don't know what to say. It feels so wrong to have these desires. It feels like betrayal to even consider admitting it. I open my mouth, but he puts a finger against my lips.

He searches my eyes for a moment before saying, "If you don't want it, I need you to bite me."

My eyes widen with surprise. "Hard?"

He shakes his head with a grin. "It doesn't have to be hard, but it needs to be obvious. They have to see it, angel. But then I can stop it and punish you instead."

I whisper, "I don't want to bite you." I don't. I don't want to be punished, and I don't want to bite him.

"I don't think it will come to that, but if it does, you have a choice." Bite me, hit me, scream at me. Do something worthy of being taken away. He gently sets his forehead against mine and kisses the tip of my nose before taking a deep breath.

"Tonight will be hard, but tomorrow may be a little harder."

"Why?" I ask. I don't understand. We should be leaving soon. Tonight is the last step, or so I thought. This is just for them to see how well he's trained me.

"I have a meeting tomorrow, and you'll have to come." I nod my head. That doesn't sound so bad.

"Just know you'll be safe. Always." His eyes are sad, and it's making me worry.

"Kade?" I don't know what the question is that's on the tip of my tongue, but whatever it is, it's hurting my chest.

"It's alright angel, I didn't mean to worry you."

"Is everything going to be okay, Kade?" I get the very strong sense that something's off.

"You're going to be fine, I promise you."

"What about you?" I ask him. Tears prick my eyes when his eyes go sad and he doesn't respond.

"Even if something happens to me, you're going to be safe. I made sure of it." Goosebumps flow down my back and I move away from Kade as he tries to pet my hair.

"You promised me that—" I don't know how to word this, but if he's not alright then he's broken his promise somehow, I know he has.

"Olivia." Kade's voice turns hard, and my eyes widen. My heart beats faster and I instantly lower myself to the floor. I stay upright on my knees and wait for him to tell me what I did wrong, just like I've done in training. Although I already know this time. The towel pools around my body, exposing my breasts to him.

Before he has a chance to admonish me, I speak the truth. "I'm scared, Kade."

His hard expression softens, and he sighs. "Come here."

I walk back into his arms, leaving the towel behind.

"I didn't mean to scare you." He kisses my hair. "I tell you too much."

I shake my head in his chest and reply, "You don't tell me enough."

He chuckles, and it eases something inside of me. I pull away from him and look into his eyes as I ask, "We're going to be okay? After tomorrow, I mean?"

I search his eyes and watch as he answers, "Of course we are. And after that we're going to leave."

Through the course of all this, I've done nothing but watch Kade as he talks with the other men at dinner. I've noticed every small detail in his expressions.

I know when he lies.

And for the first time I can recall, he just lied to me.

I wish I knew which part he was lying about.

If we're going to be okay, or if we're going to be leaving.

CHAPTER 23

Olivia

I CAN FEEL THEIR EYES ON ME AS I WALK INTO the room. Usually we come in later and the room is already full. I was expecting it to be empty when Kade said it was time to come down here. But it's not. It's already packed, and we have to walk through the crowd. My cheeks heat and my breathing comes in short pants.

They're going to watch.

I need to do this, and then we can leave. I'll be free soon. I swallow thickly and keep walking.

Kade pulls the thin chain and it tugs against the clamps on my nipples. It's a new toy, just for tonight. The slight pain sends an immediate bolt of pleasure to my clit. I'm primed to go off again already. I'm on edge and needy. He holds his hand out for me and I climb the single step onto the stage and prepare to obey my master for all of them to see.

The chains barely make any noise compared to the chatter in the room as I walk to the center of the stage. My dress is nothing but a piece of soft silk that's so thin it's nearly see-through. The delicate fabric is loose and Kade easily slips it off my shoulders, baring me to everyone.

He kisses my neck and says, "You're so beautiful." His hands caress my shoulders and his fingers linger on my body as they move down my back. I close my eyes and moan as they travel farther down and slip between my pussy lips.

"So wet, my angel," he whispers in my ear. "Do you enjoy this?" I breathe out slowly and open my eyes.

The entire crowd is watching us. The confidence I had when it was just the two of us slips.

"I don't know," I answer honestly. It's exhilarating to be up here and know they're watching. But I'm not sure I like it.

"Fair enough." He circles around me and blocks them from my view. "Are you alright?" he asks in a low voice.

I nod my head easily. I am. I can do this. A part of me is even excited to do this.

"I am, Master K." He smiles with my response and crouches down so his head is at my breast.

"Good girl," he says and looks behind him to nod at Gabriel. I swallow thickly and wait for my orders. I can do this. Just a little bit longer and I'll be free.

"You look beautiful tonight, Olivia," Gabriel says from across the room. "I have every bit of confidence in you." A flush of pride flows through me at his praise. Talia nods her head slightly, and leans onto Gabriel's leg.

"What do you say, angel?" Kade asks.

"Thank you, sir," I answer and see a flash of worry in Gabriel's eyes.

Kade's eyes find mine and hold my gaze. "Stay still, angel."

"Yes, Master K." I keep my shoulders squared and chin held high.

He crouches down with his hands on my hips and takes the clamp and my nipple in his mouth. They're sensitive and walking a razor's edge between pain and pleasure. He lowers one hand to my pussy and groans around my hardened nipple when he slips his fingers between my wet folds.

At the same time, he pushes his fingers into me and and uses his teeth to release the clamp.

"Ah!" I scream out and resist the urge to grab my breast.

The pain of the clamp being removed and the pleasure from his touch combine into something so intense I nearly collapse, but I don't. I stay as still as possible and force my eyes open. In front of me are Gabriel and Master A. Talia is in Gabriel's lap, and his hands are between her legs. He's whispering in her ear and kissing her neck as she watches Kade prepare to do the same thing to my other breast.

I hold my breath and wait for the pain to come. I stare straight ahead, focusing on the wall behind my audience and ignore their sounds. It's dark and difficult to see them anyway. I imagine we're alone.

It's just the two of us. As my orgasm builds with every stroke of Kade's fingers against my G-spot, I prepare for the pain. The only move I make is curling my toes.

Out of nowhere, Kade releases the remaining clamp and sucks my nipple as my release tears through my body. It's completely unexpected, and I scream out a strangled cry of pleasure. Kade pushes his palm against my clit and gently sucks each tender nipple until both the pleasure and pain subside.

After a long moment, I feel like I can breathe again and Kade stands in front of me. He gives me a small kiss on the shoulder and tells me to turn around. I obey him on shaky legs.

Behind me is a simple and small bench. Kade push-es gently against my lower back and I obey the unspoken command. It hits my hips and I lean over. It's bolted to the floor, and so are leather straps.

"Lean over, Olivia," he whispers in my ear. I do as I'm told. It's only a few inches wide and offers little support. He kicks the inside of my heel gently with his shoe, and I spread my legs for him. I swallow thickly as the men move around in my periphery to get a better view. I have to close my eyes as my heart races faster and he attaches a leather strap to my ankle.

"Now your wrists," Kade says before kissing my thigh. I look back at him, not understanding. We've never done this before.

"Bend further, angel." My blood heats as I lower my shoulders and lean down so my hands nearly touch the floor. The thin bench keeps my ass in the air. It's only then that I realize the padding on it is for my hips.

My breath comes in shallow pants as he buckles the straps tightly around my wrists. They're a few inches long so I have a little give, but not much. And with that, I'm bound and bent over, completely bared for all of them to see. I'm completely vulnerable and relying fully on my trust in Kade. My anxiety peaks.

I feel Kade's hand on my lower back and that's the only warning I get before he slams into me from behind.

"Uh!" I bite down on my bottom lip as Kade pounds into me. His fingers dig into my hips. Over and over again he thrusts all the way into me. He's so deep. Each time is so deep. I almost can't stand it.

"Let them hear you," Kade says loudly as his hand grips the nape of my neck. "Let them hear how loud you are when I fuck you like this."

"Fuck!" I close my eyes as he tears through me without mercy. I have to be careful. I can't scream out his name, Kade. Master K. Master K. I have to remember. But fuck! My toes curl and my legs tremble as he pushes in and out of me repeatedly with a relentless pace.

"Yes!" He pushes against my clit and I spasm around him as my mouth falls open and I cum violently. My body heats as the pleasure pulses through me. My vision goes black as Kade pumps into me a few more times before pulling out completely. I keep my back straight and hold that position as he circles me.

I see his dick in front of me covered in my arousal and I anticipate him pushing his large cock down my throat, but he doesn't.

He cups my chin in his hand and he brings my lips to his. It's a struggle to maintain this position with my wrists bound, but I do it. My breathing comes in shallow pants as he crushes his lips against mine. His tongue dips into my mouth and massages mine. It's a passionate, yet dark dance that makes my heart beat faster. He breaks the kiss and nips my bottom lip before releasing me.

I fall some, but I pull myself back up. My wrists pull against the shackles as I keep my upper body nearly parallel with the floor.

Kade moves behind me and again the only warning I get is his lower hand on my back, right before he slams into me. My arousal drips down my leg as he continues the punishing fuck. Over and over. Each time, he gives me my release.

By the time he's done with me, my legs won't stop shaking and I'm out of breath completely, barely able to hold myself upright. I do though. I push through the trembling need to pass out and stand tall once the shackles are removed. Kade rubs my wrists and ankles, kissing them each before moving on to the next.

He takes enough time doing so that I finally feel centered and as though I can continue.

Kade leads me to the exit of the stage and I look at his back with hesitation. The performance generally lasts for hours. It hasn't been that long. Has it? I follow him without question although I'm feeling uncertain. My cheeks are burning furiously with a blush as we walk past the onlookers.

Before we leave the room, Kade pauses at the exit and waits for Gabriel and Master A.

Talia's nearly passed out in Gabriel's arms. Judging from the blush on her chest and cheeks, she's sated as well.

"I need to put my Talia to bed." Gabriel walks easily with her in his arms. "I'll meet you three in just a minute."

My eyes widen as I take in the meaning of his words.

It's not over yet.

CHAPTER 24

Olivia

I SIT ON MY KNEES IN THE QUIET AND DIMLY LIT office. My hands rest on my thighs and my eyes are on the floor. I can hear the ice cubes clinking in Gabriel's glass as he lifts it to his lips. I'm trying to breathe, but it's hard.

"Relax, Olivia." I still don't know his real name. Master A. I've seen him so many times now, but I have no idea what his name is.

I stare into his eyes, willing myself to come up with a

response, but I can't. I can hardly breathe. I swallow thickly and part my lips, but still nothing.

Kade's hand settles on my shoulder and I instantly close my eyes. My tense body relaxes.

"Come sit in my lap," Master A says as he pats his legs with both of his hands. I look up at Kade over my shoulders. I don't know what to do. I thought I was only supposed to listen to Kade.

His eyes are on Master A. He cocks a brow and then looks back down at me.

"Go ahead, angel. I'm right here."

I slowly rise and walk to Master A. He leans forward and grips my hips, pulling me down onto his lap before I have a chance to sit.

I let out a small gasp, and the men in the room chuckle.

"Be honest with me, Olivia," Master A says in my ear. His hot breath greets my neck and I lean my head so he has more access to the tender skin.

He groans and rocks his dick against my ass. "I'm trying to be good here."

Kade lets out a small laugh and leans forward, resting his elbows on his knees. "She makes it hard to resist."

Master A runs a hand down his face before pulling my small body closer to his chest. "Are you scared, or just nervous?" he asks loud enough for everyone in the room to hear.

Nervous. I'm so fucking nervous.

I lick my lips and answer him honestly. "Nervous."

He groans in my neck and presses his lips against my skin. "Thank fuck," he says as his hands slip up the sheer fabric of my dress. His fingers slowly rise on my inner thighs until they're almost pressed against my core.

My eyes dart to Kade's. My lips part and my back bows slightly, moving away from Master A.

"It's alright, angel." Kade's watching us intently.

I don't know if I should believe him. This feels wrong.

"What's my name, Olivia?" Gabriel asks from across the room as he sets his glass down.

"For tonight," Kade says with a hard edge. I look between the two men with slight anxiety.

Master A chuckles in my ear as his thumbs slip closer up to my clit.

Kade looks me in the eyes and asks, "What are you going to call them tonight, Olivia?"

The meaning of Gabriel's question hits me with clarity. "Master," I whisper.

"Say it louder," Kade demands. "I want them to hear you calling them Master." He turns back to Gabriel and repeats, "For tonight."

Gabriel grins and says, "I understand." His eyes find mine. "You're *ours* tonight." My pussy clenches, and Master A nips my ear.

"You like that, don't you?" Master A asks me. Yes. A part of me does. The idea is so forbidden and exotic, and I want it. But I want Kade more. I don't want to ruin whatever this is between us. I *need* him.

I nervously look back to Kade again. I move my hand to reach out to him and then put it back on the sofa.

"Stop." Kade's hard voice echoes off the walls.

Master A looks up at him, letting a chill blow in the crook of my neck and slowly rests his back against the chair, leaving me sitting nervously on top of his lap.

"Come here," he demands. His words are hard. His chest rises and falls with his steady breathing. The idea I've upset him makes my blood race with adrenaline and anxiety. I slowly slip off Master A's lap. He holds my hand until I'm steady on my feet.

I keep my eyes on the ground as I walk over to Kade. Even if he's angry with me, that's okay so long as I'm still his. I start to lower myself to the ground in front of him, but he stops me.

"Over here, angel." My eyes fly to his at his soft words. He pats the armrest of the sofa. I walk to the side of it and he holds his hand out. I slip mine into his and he gently tugs. My hips butt against the arm of the chair and my upper body falls into his lap.

He brushes the hair away from my face and rests his arm over my lower back. He rubs gently as Gabriel and

Master A rise from their seats one after the other. Kade lifts my dress and exposes my pussy to them.

"Look at me, angel." I lift my head and wait with bated breath.

"Now would be the time to say no if you don't want this." His eyes hold mine, and I can tell neither of us are breathing.

I hear a zipper and the sound of the men walking closer. My lips part as I search Kade's eyes.

He grips the hair at the base of my skull and lifts my head up. My pussy clenches with the slight pain. He lowers his lips to mine and takes them with his own. I moan into his lips as hands grip my hips and tilt them slightly. My eyes pop wide open.

My heart stills as my pussy clenches around nothing.

This is really going to happen. Holy fuck!

Kade gives me a smirk. "I'll be right here." He leans back and gives a nod to whoever's behind me.

"She's so fucking wet, I think you've been depriving her, Master K." I recognize Master A's voice. He tightens his grip on one hip and uses the other to stroke his dick. I jump forward slightly as the head of his dick pushes through my pussy lips, running up and down before slipping deeper into my hot entrance.

I turn my head to look back at Kade.

His mouth is parted, and his heated gaze stares back

at me. I bite down on my bottom lip to hold in the noises threatening to leave my lips, and Master A pushes deeper inside me.

Gabriel's voice rings out as a hand smacks against my ass. "Spread." The stinging pain is directly connected to my clit and the mix of pain and pleasure makes me moan. I quickly spread my legs apart wider and look to Kade for approval. He pets my back and plants a kiss on my shoulders.

"Oh fuck, you're so tight." Master A's hands slip under my hips and he pulls me back some. He slowly pulls out and then pushes back in, stretching my walls.

A heavy breath leaves my lips as he moves in and out of me slowly.

"Open your mouth, Olivia." I turn my head at the sound of Gabriel's voice to my right, and my eyes widen. My body jolts as Master A picks up his pace. Gabriel rests his right knee on the sofa, bringing his body closer to me. Gabriel grips his thick cock and strokes it once before smacking it against my cheek. "Open."

I part my lips and open as wide as I can to fit him. He pushes his massive girth past my lips and I try to cover my teeth with my lips. "So fucking good," he says.

Gabriel groans, pulling my hair into a ponytail with his fist. His other hand grips my throat to keep me still. All the while Kade rubs soothing circles on my lower back. Gabriel pushes in deeper, so deep I have to breathe through my nose. My body heats with the pleasure of being used and filled. Master A slaps my ass as he pounds into me. His balls slap against my clit with each thrust.

Gabriel pushes in deeper, and I feel like I'm going to choke. I try to hold it back though and continue to breathe through my nose. A long moment passes as Master A thrusts behind me, pushing me deeper and deeper onto Gabriel's dick before he pulls out of my mouth. I take in a breath and dig my fingers into Kade's thigh, trying desperately to hold on. I'm at a steep edge of heightened pleasure.

Gabriel reaches behind me, and I'm not sure why. His hand slips between the armrest and my pussy. He ruthlessly rubs my clit and Kade holds me down as my body thrashes with my impending release. My body feels so hot. Too hot. My legs shake, and Master A only fucks me harder and faster.

"Cum for him now," Kade commands me, and I obey.

My pussy squeezes around his dick as the intense pleasure rolls through my body, but before it's done, before the waves let up, Master A pulls out of me completely and Gabriel takes his place, thrusting all of himself deep inside me.

"Fuck!" I scream out.

"Good girl," Kade says as I hear Master A groaning. Kade's hands leave me for the first time as Gabriel fucks me with a force so hard, it's nearly too much. Gabriel adjusts me so he can get in deeper and I let out a strangled cry. He's pushing me to the point of pain. My arousal leaks down my thighs and my clit rubs against the armrest with every forceful thrust.

My body feels so hot. My hands fly to Kade's arms for support, I need him.

"It's alright, angel." His voice is unsteady and full of lust. Gabriel pulls me away from Kade enough that Kade can reach his pants. I grip onto the armrest, realizing he's not leaving me. I try to pick my body up enough for him to unleash his cock, but Gabriel's thrusts are so hard, I'm jolted forward.

Gabriel reaches his arm around to my front, bracing my body on his forearm. He slows his pace slightly and leans down, kissing my shoulder as Kade strokes his dick.

"You feel so good, Olivia," Gabriel says before moving away and slowly letting his arm slide down my body until he's only gripping my hip.

Kade moves his dick to my lips and I eagerly take him in my mouth. His hand fists in my hair, but he doesn't control my movements. I anticipate him pushing my head down or bucking his hips, but he doesn't. I massage his dick with my tongue as I push my head down and move up and down his length.

I pull back, letting Kade's dick pop out of my mouth as Gabriel thrusts deep inside me and stills. I scream out from the intense sensation. My pussy pulses around him, and my body trembles with pleasure. My legs are so weak they give out, but Gabriel's hold on my hips keeps me upright.

Kade gently moves me back to him. I suck on his dick and hollow my cheeks as I do everything I can to get him off.

Gabriel's fucking me so deep and hard, I know I'm going to lose it any second. I resist and hold on, wanting to cum with Kade.

He hisses with pleasure as I shove him down my throat as deep as I can and try to swallow. My eyes sting and I can't breathe, but I'm as desperate for his release as I am my own.

It only takes a few minutes until Kade groans and bucks his hips, once, twice, and then a third time. Hot jets of his cum shoot in the back of my throat, and I swallow as quickly as I can.

Gabriel pulls out and all I can hear is his heavy breathing as he furiously strokes himself until he's reached his own climax. His hot cum splashes on my lower back as I swallow Kade's and wipe my mouth and find my release with them. The numbing pleasure wrecks my body, but both men keep me still with their firm grip on me. I'm breathless and exhausted. I lower my chest against Kade's thigh and hold on to him as I close my eyes.

Gabriel leans down and plants kisses along my spine that leave a chill. I shiver slightly and smile when I hear him chuckle.

I'm barely aware of what's going on around me. I jump slightly as Gabriel wipes my lower back clean and Kade instantly pulls me into his arms. My body is still trembling.

Kade holds me close to his chest as I come down from the intense orgasm. I shift in his lap and the movement makes my clit pulse with a sated need. I bury my head into Kade's chest and moan. But I'm spent. I can't take anymore. Exhaustion weighs heavy on me.

I feel a hand push my hair away from my face. I hesitantly look up as Master A leans down. He plants a small kiss on my forehead. A violent blush hits my cheeks as he looks down on me.

His lips kick up into a smirk and he says, "If you ever want a new Master, you just let me know."

Kade huffs a laugh. "You must have a death wish."

"Sleep well, Olivia," Gabriel says from across the room as he opens the door. He nods at Kade, and Master A walks toward the door.

The door closes behind them and Kade kisses my hair.

My heart beats a bit faster realizing it's over. I slowly raise my eyes to meet his and when they do, I feel nothing but comfort.

He has a soft smile on his lips. "Are you alright, angel?" he asks.

I nod my head and move my hands to his chest. The

tips of my fingers play with a small bit of chest hair peeking through his shirt.

He lowers his head to the crook of my neck and whispers in my ear, "I enjoyed that more than I should have."

I bury my head under his chin to hide the grin growing on my lips. A strange sense of pride washes over me.

But then something changes, the fantasy and illusion that seems to slip into place when I'm with Kade and in need shatters, and I feel lost and vulnerable. I shouldn't be enjoying this. I shouldn't feel *loved*. He doesn't love me. I can't love him.

But I do. Not only do I feel loved by him, I'm painfully aware in this moment that I love Kade.

CHAPTER 25

Olivia

KADE TAKES A SEAT IN THE SMALL SITTING room and I obediently kneel next to him. I'm not sure what this meeting is about, but I want it to be over with. I haven't forgotten our conversation, and I'm ready to get over this hurdle so we can leave.

Master A walks into the room, and my breathing is caught short. My cheeks burn as he walks past me. He takes a seat in the chair next to Kade so that I'm kneeling on the floor between the two of them.

"Good morning, angel," Master A says with a wink. Talia giggles from her position on the other side of the room.

"Good morning, Mast-sir. Good morning, sir!" Master A claps his hands once and bellows out a laugh.

"I will kill you. Don't think I won't," Kade says from my right. I look up at him and he has a sexy smile on his face. He places his hand on the outside of my shoulder and scoots me closer to him. I settle between his legs and lean my head against his knee. I look at Master A from the corner of my eye, and he winks at me.

A small smile graces my lips. That warmth in my chest comes back, but I wish it didn't.

I wish I didn't feel so comfortable here.

Gabriel comes back into the room and a young woman follows him. Her simple strapless black dress flows as she walks quickly behind him. Her short hair is nearly as black as her dress.

"Alright then, let's try this out."

In the center of the sitting room is a device I've never seen before. It's a simple rope pulley although the ropes themselves are woven with gold chains with cuffs on the end. The pulley is already set up and dangling from the ceiling. Gabriel lowers the cuffs with the rope, and the young woman stands and instantly raises her arms.

"There's no support?" Kade asks with uncertainty. I look at Master A, and he has his forehead pinched and his jaw is clenched.

"Lydia will let us know how it feels," Gabriel answers smoothly.

Master A sits back in his seat. "I'm sure it'll only be for the red rooms."

Gabriel nods his head. "And that's why Lydia's testing it out, and not my Talia."

Gabriel walks to the rope after fastening the cuffs and slowly pulls. Lydia's arms are pulled upward until she's on her tiptoes. Her body sways, but being held up so high, she can't balance herself with just her big toes. Gabriel lowers it slightly and waits for her to steady herself, then raises it higher again.

"How do you like it?" he asks her.

Master A cocks a brow as the small woman answers, "It would hurt after a while, but for a quick fuck, it'll do the job." Gabriel lets out a rough chuckle.

"We'll have to get a few then." He looks at his watch as a loud chime rings out. Talia stands and exits gracefully. She doesn't wait for orders. The rules between her and Gabriel are much different than they are for everyone else.

"Fifteen minutes then?" Gabriel looks up at Lydia, who nods her head and answers simply, "Yes, sir."

I don't want to get in that thing. That's all I can think about as Gabriel pushes against Lydia's hip and she swings slightly. Her big toes slide across the rug as she lets out a squeak and then a laugh.

"It could be fun," Gabriel says with a smile. The room feels light with laughter. It does look... interesting, but I have zero arm strength and that looks like it would tire me out quickly.

The laughter dies the second Talia returns to the room. Her head is down and her hands are clasped in front of her as she returns to her seat on the floor in front of Gabriel's empty chair.

Vic follows her into the room and stands in the doorway.

Ice pricks down my skin as he looks at the woman dangling.

Lydia's smile slips, and she goes silent as Gabriel steadies her.

"Victor. I wasn't expecting you so soon," Gabriel says. I keep my eyes trained on the ground as Victor walks across the floor. His black boots thumping across the ground are the only sounds until he slumps in Gabriel's seat. He spreads his legs wide and his boot hits Talia's leg. She doesn't move and simply allows it.

My eyes dart to Gabriel's. He's staring fixedly at his foot.

My breathing picks up and anxiety ignites within me. I can't see all the men's faces, but the tension in the air is thick.

"What's this?" Victor asks. His voice is low and rough. He gestures with his hand although he seems bored.

"A new toy we're considering installing." I watch as

Victor stands and pushes the small woman. Lydia's silent as she swings and struggles to steady herself. Her hands wrap around the rope to support her weight since her toes are no longer touching the ground.

Vic huffs a laugh and then he walks closer to me.

"Kade."

"Victor." Kade replies with the same temperament, cold and disinterested.

"Ricky wanted to know how you were handling the gift." I can see past Victor's legs and Gabriel seems to be having a silent discussion with Talia. Gabriel looks back toward my direction, his eyes on Victor as he walks to a side table and opens a drawer. I watch as he lays a gun on the side table. My heart speeds up faster, but he leaves it there and continues to watch.

"Ricky could've called and asked himself."

"I wanted to come and see for myself. She should be trained by now, shouldn't she?"

"She is." Kade rests his hand on my head and gently pets my hair, but it does nothing to calm me. "As you can see."

"Fantastic. I've been ready to fuck this little bitch since we caught her."

"You'll have to get in line then, Victor," Gabriel says from across the room. "I'll call first dibs." Gabriel's trying to keep the mood light, but it doesn't work.

"What the fuck does that mean?" Victor asks.

"She's mine. That's what the fuck it means. And I'm not willing to share her just yet."

Victor clenches his fist like a petulant brat, but then seems to calm himself.

"How about you come with me to the meet in a few days?" Victor offers. "You can get rid of this one and get yourself some fresh stock?" It's difficult to stay still as he talks about me as though I'm disposable. My heart clenches in my chest and I have to remind myself this is fake. I'll be free soon. Very soon. I breathe in deep. I just need to stay calm.

"You can pass her to me then. Once you've had your fill." Kade makes no move to respond as Victor stands and takes a few steps toward me with confidence. I keep my eyes on the ground, but my body trembles with the need to run.

"For now, I'll just see how well she obeys." His voice takes on a hard edge, but then he says easily, "Just to let Ricky know how well you've done. *If* you've trained her right."

I don't want to. I consider turning around and biting the shit out of Kade's knee or doing anything I can to get out of this. I don't want to obey Victor. I don't trust him. I don't want anything to do with him. It's more than that though. I'm terrified.

"Within this room, I give you permission to give her simple commands," Kade says.

"Simple commands?" Victor sneers. "And you expect me not to leave the room?" He snorts and looks to Master A for support, but judging by how his face falls, he obviously didn't get any support from Master A.

"She's *mine*." My body tenses at Kade's hard words although his claim on me affects me differently. "She is not to leave my sight."

I can feel Victor's eyes on me in the silence. I remain still and wait with bated breath.

"Come on then. Crawl to me," Victor commands me. I don't want to. I hesitate even though I know I shouldn't.

"Go on, angel," Kade finally says, and I feel betrayed. I don't want to. "You can do this." Kade's voice is soft. I swallow thickly and nod my head.

"Bow and kiss my boots, slave," Victor says with a smug confidence in his voice as I crawl toward him. I'm afraid to. The thought that he's going to kick me in my face is a very real fear of mine. But I do it. I crawl to him and bow on the floor and put a kiss on each boot before laying my head down next to his feet and waiting.

"She's a wonderful pet," Kade says from behind me "Very easy to train." I don't like the way he's talking. This is a different side to him; one I've never seen. I want to believe it's fake. But I don't know for sure. My heart tries to climb up my throat, but I swallow it down and continue to wait to be commanded by this man I detest.

I hear Victor unzip his pants and my eyes pop wide open. I can't do this. I won't. I won't let this fucker touch me.

"You will not use for her anything other than simple commands. I'm not in the habit of sharing." Kade sounds pissed.

I can practically see Victor's sick smile. "I have no plans to touch her." He sounds casual and cocky.

"If you cum on my property," Kade's voice is even but deadly, "I'll slit your throat."

I chance a look up. Victor's dark eyes stare back at Kade who's still seated behind me, and I can see he's weighing his options.

"What good is she then?" he asks with disdain.

Victor snorts and steps over me, moving to the woman dangling in the center of the room.

"Come here now," Kade commands me to crawl to him and I try to obey and crawl back to him, but the loud smack of Victor's hand against Lydia's body stops me.

Lydia whimpers as I look up and see her body swinging from the ropes.

"Victor!" Gabriel calls out a low warning. "This is in testing, and she's not prepared for you."

Victor completely ignores Gabriel. I keep my eyes on the ground, but I can see Gabriel stand and walk toward the center of the room. My heart thumps loudly in my ears.

"Don't fucking disrespect me, *Master G.*" Victor taunts Gabriel by using the name we call him. Victor's pissed and apparently done with listening to anyone. "This bitch is a whore, and I'll fuck her like a whore."

Everything happens too quickly. Gabriel moves to the ropes and Master A to Talia, standing in front of her.

Gabriel yells something in French I don't understand and Lydia cries out.

Victor's hurting her, grabbing her roughly toward him and yanking her arms against the rope. My heart lurches in my chest and I instinctively reach out to stop him. Fear and disgust cripple me, but I fight them and reach out to grab Victor's leg. I can't let him do that. Kade grabs my hips and pulls me away, my fingers barely touching Victor's pants and doing nothing to stop him. I hear him yelling. The other men yelling. Lydia's crying. The horrific chaos hits me at once.

One moment is clear though. Victor looks down at me with a sick, twisted smile and pulls Lydia even closer to him with a violent yank. My heart refuses to beat, and time moves in slow motion.

Lydia screams as Victor pulls her. She screams a sound of horrid pain as I hear a loud *pop* and her arm pulls from the socket in her shoulder even though the rope is being lowered. Gabriel was too late. Her upper body drops, but her arm is limp at her side.

Kade picks me up swiftly and moves me behind him and onto the chair. I'm disgusted and want to do something. I have to try to help her.

I watch as Kade reaches into his waistband, but before he can pull out his gun, my body jolts with each loud sound of a gun going off. *Bang! Bang!*

My head whips to the side and I see Talia holding the gun, pointed right where Victor was standing. Her body is still as Victor falls lifeless to the floor. His cold dark eyes stare at the ceiling. His face is contorted, and blood bubbles from a neat hole in his throat. His dark black shirt sticks to his body as blood spills from the wound in his chest.

My eyes stay on him, until I hear the pounding of footsteps and a squeak from Talia.

Gabriel grabs Talia by her throat, stopping her from kneeling. The gun falls from her hand and hits the ground with a loud thump.

"You will not hide behind your submission, Talia." Gabriel sounds pissed. Talia lets out a small sob and keeps her eyes on the ground.

"Get her down." Gabriel's low voice sends the command throughout the room. He's not talking to Talia, but I'm not sure who the order was directed toward.

My eyes are still locked on Talia's face. She's scared. It's the first time I've seen her look unsure and upset. It's also the first time he's scolded her. And for what? Killing a man who deserves to die? Blood pools around his neck and seeps into the carpet.

Kade moves to go to Lydia, but I grip onto his leg. I don't want him to leave me. Kade looks down at me registering my needs, and then to Master A. Master A stands and quickly moves to Lydia, unfastening the cuffs and cradles her in his arms. He shushes her and carries her out of the room.

Kade pulls me off the ground and holds me to his chest. He tries calming me, he tries keeping me from looking at Talia and Gabriel, but I turn away from him.

The only sound in the rom is Talia's soft cry. She doesn't deserve to be crying.

"*Esclave*, did you think I would let him get away with that? Do you think that little of me now?" His voice is low.

"No Master," Talia replies quickly.

My heart hurts for her. I move to push away from Kade. I'm not going to watch her be punished for doing the right thing, but he digs his fingers into my hips, stopping me.

Gabriel loosens his grip on Talia's throat and cups her chin. "You will never put yourself in danger again. Do you hear me?" Gabriel's voice is soft, but absolute.

She finally looks into his eyes and sniffles.

"Answer me, *esclave*." Gabriel's eyes dart across her face, searching for something.

"If you want something done, you will tell me. You will not make yourself a target, ever." His voice raises with each command. "Is that clear? You will stand behind me always. Don't you ever do that again."

My breathing slows as I understand why he's upset. My anger wanes, and the fight in me dies.

"It's alright, angel," Kade whispers, pulling me closer to him and petting my back.

Talia nods her head and hunches her shoulders. "Yes, Master."

Gabriel pulls her into his arms. "Don't you dare do that again, Talia," he whispers in her hair and then kisses her. He rubs his hand along her back as she sniffles.

I watch as he soothes her pain and both of them relax slightly. He doesn't stop looking at her and wills her to look at him, but she buries her face into his chest.

It's quiet for a long time. I want to leave. I want to get out of here.

Kade finally breaks the silence. "She has very good aim," he says to Gabriel.

Gabriel turns toward us and huffs a laugh. "Just because she can shoot doesn't mean she should. I was taking care of it."

Talia looks at the ground with a frown and wipes her eyes. "I'm sorry," she says. She sounds so weak.

Gabriel pulls away from her and grips her shoulders. "Don't be, *esclave*." He comforts her. "Try to stay behind me next time," he says in a soft, comforting tone.

She nods her head and asks in a small voice, "Are you mad at me still?"

He shakes his head and plants a soft kiss on her lips. Gabriel whispers, "Never. I love you, *esclave*."

She buries her head into his chest and whispers, "I love you, Gabriel."

Gabriel rubs her back and looks over his shoulder at us.

I pull my eyes away from them and lower my cheek to Kade's chest.

"I'll take her upstairs and come down to clean this up," Kade says. Gabriel looks back at us and then down to the dead body on the floor. "Victor was never here. We need to make sure Ricky doesn't find out."

Kade's deep voice rumbles in his chest. "Of course not. He was never here."

CHAPTER 26

Olivia

"I WANT TO LEAVE, KADE." THAT'S ALL I'VE been thinking since this morning. I can't sleep. I'm wide awake, lying on the bed. I've been in this room all day while Kade's been gone 'cleaning up that mess', as he referred to it.

I keep seeing Victor's lifeless eyes.

I'm not okay.

"Soon, angel." I shake my head as Kade dries off his hair and drops the towel on the floor.

I was quiet when he came back in. I laid still in bed while he got undressed and went to shower. But I'm not okay. I can't just be quiet and wait for him anymore.

I need to get out of here.

"I can't stay here any longer."

He walks to the bed and stands in front of me. Just being close to him again calms a part of me, but I'm still ready to bolt. I'm done waiting

Kade climbs on the bed and cups my chin in his hand, lifting my eyes so I have to stare into his. It's a motion he does often and usually I lean into his touch, but not now.

He starts to speak, but I interrupt him.

"I've never seen a dead man up close before. I can't. I can't stop seeing it. And the way he looked at me." I shake my head nearly violently as the fear comes back, squeezing my lungs of their breath.

"You'll be alright, angel. I'm here now." His voice has that calming tone he uses with me, but I don't want to be calmed down.

He walks to the bed and takes a seat next to me. Just being close to him again calms a part of me, but I'm still not okay.

"I'm sorry I had to leave you today. I would have stayed, but I had to take care of that."

His eyes search mine, but I can't give him the acceptance I know he wants. I can't cave into him. I need to leave.

"The only other person I've ever seen die is the man you killed that night, and—" Before I can finish, Kade leaves me. He quickly sits up from the bed and turns his back to me, reaching for the towel on the floor and going back to the bathroom.

My body stiffens. "Kade?" I call out for him and move the sheets off of me as I scoot closer to the edge.

He's never done that before, just leave me like that. I start to question my resolve. I think back on what I said and I regret saying it all, although I don't know why. I don't want him to leave me.

As the time passes and he doesn't respond, my heart beats faster with worry. I can't lose him. I need him.

I let out a breath as he comes back into the room. He doesn't seem mad or upset. I part my lips to ask him what I said, but I'm afraid to. I wait for him.

"I'm sorry I've done such a horrible thing to you, angel," he says with sincerity as he comes back into the room. "I promise I'll take care of you. I'll make this right." His voice is firm. But something's wrong. He's holding something back from me.

"What's wrong?" I ask hesitantly. I've never seen him like this before. Fear overwhelms me. "Did Ricky find out?"

Kade shakes his head. "I wish I could tell you. I want to

tell you everything." He bends down and kisses me. "Ask me for something I can give you. Anything."

"I want to leave."

He lowers his head, his forehead pressed to mine and sighs. My heart sinks in my hollow chest.

"I will never let any of them hurt you." He speaks barely above a murmur.

"He did hurt me though. Victor hurt me." Kade's eyes close tighter as I continue my plea. "I don't want this anymore. I can't do that again." I don't know how to explain it to him.

I can't do that again. I don't want to. I don't want any of this anymore.

"I'm sorry. That was a mistake. I thought it would prevent things from getting out of hand." He takes a deep breath. "I thought wrong."

I don't know what to say to him.

"I'm sorry, angel." His soft blue eyes look deep into mine. "Please forgive me, tell me you'll forgive me."

My heart swells with the need to soothe his pain. I don't like seeing him like this. "I forgive you."

Kade's lips press gently against mine the second the words leave my lips. I moan softly, accepting his gentle touch. His hands move to my lower back and mine spear into his hair. A calmness settles over me. This is what I need. I need Kade.

Kade breaks our kiss and looks at me with a spark of lust in his eyes.

"Lie back," Kade commands me, and although a part of me doesn't want to, I obey.

My breath is shaky as Kade grips my hips and pulls me to the edge of the bed.

"Relax, angel. I've got you." I put a hand over my face, trying to calm myself as he spreads my knees farther. I'm a mix of emotions and I feel as though I'm being pulled in too many different directions. He lowers his lips to my pussy and my body shudders as he takes a languid lick.

I'm not prepared for him, not like I usually am. My head falls to the side as he sucks my clit into his mouth.

I heat for him instantly and close my eyes with a small moan. My fingertips dig into the mattress, and I have to work hard to keep my body still. I want to wrap my legs around his head and rock my pussy into his face. But I don't.

I stay still and let him do with me as he wants. His large hands grip my ass and angle me for him. He spears his tongue and fucks me with it over and over. My mouth falls open as my belly stirs with desire and need.

He takes me to the edge and I'm almost there, but this isn't what I need. I need *him*.

"More, please." I do something I've never done. I reach down and pull him on his shoulders. I need to feel him. I need to be as close to him as possible.

My eyes widen as I realize what I did, but the heat in Kade's eyes as he climbs over my body erases the momentary fear of acting out. He pulls me across the bed under him and devours my lips with his.

I can faintly taste myself on his tongue, but I don't care. My hands travel up his muscular body and I wrap my legs around his hips. He moans into my mouth and moves his hard dick to my opening, pushing in slowly.

His girth stretches my walls and I throw my head back and moan into the cool air. His lips suck at my neck as he pushes himself deeper inside of me. He stills deep inside of me, buried to the hilt, and captures my lips. It's almost too much. I feel so full and desperate for him to move. He doesn't though.

He kisses me as though he needs the air in my lungs to breathe.

I feel his passion, and it consumes me. His hands grip my hips tighter and he pulls out for a moment and then slams into me. Fuck! My mouth pops open with a silent scream. It's so good, but too overwhelming. His eyes stare into mine as he does it again and again.

Each hard pump heightens the edge of my release. My body tenses and heats.

"Kade," I whimper, and that's his undoing. A low growl erupts from his chest and he buries his head in the crook of my neck as he fucks me relentlessly into the mattress.

He pounds into me over and over again. Each hard thrust smacks against my clit and makes my body that much hotter.

My head thrashes, and my fingernails dig into his shoulders. I struggle not to cry out.

"Mine," he growls into my neck.

My eyes close and my head falls back as he fucks me harder, owning my body with each hard thrust.

"Mine." He nips my neck and then my shoulder.

I can't contain the strangled scream of pleasure as he pushes my legs out wider and thrusts deeper inside of me, pushing me to a point of slight pain that's overwhelmed with pleasure.

"Kade!" I scream his name as he loses control and ruts between my legs with a savage need. My lungs refuse to work as my temperature rises, and waves of pleasure rock through my body with a paralyzing force. My mouth opens with a silent scream and Kade's quick to bite my bottom lip and then my throat as he rides through my orgasm, racing for his own release.

He stills deep inside of me and groans from deep within his chest. He thrusts short, shallow pumps that only seem to prolong my orgasm. My body shudders with a chill as he pulls out of me and leaves me for a moment. I feel overwhelmed with a hot, tingling sensation rippling through my body in waves.

The aftershocks dim as Kade wipes between my legs with a warm cloth and I settle into the mattress.

Kade holds me close to him. His warmth settles into every part of me, calming me and letting me relax into the bed.

A calmness washes over me and I begin to think that everything will be alright, but then Kade's phone beeps from the nightstand. He pulls away from me, rolling onto his back and picking it up. I miss him instantly. I need him to come back to me, but he doesn't. I watch his face as he looks at the message.

The softness in his features vanishes and the cold façade returns.

He gets up from the bed without saying a word and walks to his dresser.

I slowly sit up and watch as he dresses himself.

"Kade?" I ask him. He can't leave me. I need him.

He looks at me as he pulls his pants up and zips and buttons them, but he doesn't say anything..

"Are you alright?"

"I'm fine, angel. Go to bed." I can tell from his voice he's not fine. A weight settles against my chest, threatening to suffocate me.

"Kade, please don't leave me." I pull the covers tight around me and up to my chest. I don't want to be left alone.

He walks to the bed and gives me a look of sympathy

mixed with something else... longing. It's a look of longing. He plants a soft kiss on my lips and I move my hand to the back of his head to deepen it, but he pulls away before I'm able to.

"I'm sorry, angel." His thumb brushes along my cheek and then he leaves me.

I stare at the door, waiting for him to come back. Unable to sleep, and unable to stop seeing the longing in his eyes.

CHAPTER 27

Kade

I SIT ACROSS THE DESK FROM GABRIEL. HE'S AT ease, and I'm tense.

I need to get her out of here. The text confirmed what my handler said two days ago. I'm fucked, and I can deal with those consequences. But not my angel. I need to get her safely away as soon as possible.

He picks up his glass and takes another sip. He cocks a brow at me as he sets the glass down and asks, "Are you

sure you don't want one? You look as though you need it."
His voice holds the same humor I see sparkling in his eyes.

I shake my head and clear my throat, finally spitting out
the reason I'm here. "I need you to take Olivia." I have to
leave. I have to go to this meeting tomorrow. But she can't
come. She needs to be safe by noon tomorrow. And I need
Gabriel's help. I fucking hate that I do, but I have no one
else to ask. I've played my cards all wrong. And now I'm a
dead man.

"You can't be serious, Kade. You don't want her?" he
asks incredulously.

I'm quick to shake my head. Gabriel continues speaking
as I try to find the right words without giving him too much
information. He's going to find out sooner or later.

"I care for Olivia, but it would hurt my Talia. I know it
would. I don't understand why you don't want her."

I do want her. I want Olivia more than anything. I wish
I could take her and run away with her. But I can't. I can't
put her in danger. And I'm right in the middle of it. I need to
get her away from me. I need to know she's safe.

"I have to leave tomorrow, and I don't think it's safe to
take her with me." I tell him the truth. I wish I'd planned
what to say to him. But I have no plan. Just the urgency
to make sure she'll be alright. I shake my head, trying to
figure out how to tell him without giving him too much
information. He's going to find out sooner or later. If I leave

now, they could follow me. Intel is sure it's just Ricky that knows. But I don't trust him or anyone who works for him. He could have men here or others on the way. I can't risk her getting caught in a shootout. I need protection while I get her to a safe place. Or for someone else to do it.

"You're going to have to be more specific then, Kade." Gabriel's patience is waning.

"I need her to go home." I hold his firm gaze. "I need her to be safe." That's all he needs to know.

Gabriel purses his lips for a moment and knocks his knuckles against the desk.

"You need to tell me what's going on before I agree to anything." Gabriel lowers his voice, and I see distrust in his eyes. Fuck, I don't want to tell him. I need him to do this regardless. I trust him. I *know* him. I know he'll do the right thing for her. He'll help her. Even if he slits my throat, I know he'll help her. He's done it before. I know he will. And I have no other choice.

"I'll tell you. I'll tell you everything. Just promise me that you'll find a way for her to get home."

"You're going to leave her in that condition, Kade?" he sneers. "You broke her, and now you're sending her back?" He sounds disgusted.

"She's not broken," I respond evenly.

"You're delusional if you think that."

"They're going to kill me, Gabriel, I have no choice." My

body trembles with anger, but also fear for her. I can't tell him the truth until he promises me. "You've done it before. You've given them their freedom before."

"So you want me to take her home because someone's going to kill you?" Gabriel asks with disbelief.

I nod my head once. "But only if I can't. I don't know how much time I have."

"And can I ask why you're so sure you're going to die?" he asks.

I stare into his eyes. "Because Stone is going to kill me."

"I never quite liked Stone." He taps his fingers on the desk again and looks past me as if he's debating something. Are you going to tell me why?" he asks.

"She has nothing to do with this." My blood rushes in my ears. "You'll help me take her home regardless of what happens between us?" Although it's a question, it comes out as a statement.

His eyes finally meet mine. "I will." He nods his head with certainty.

"Whatever you want to do to me when you find out, it'll be on hold until she's safe." He nods his head once again, keeping my gaze.

"I'm a man of my word, Kade. Now out with it."

My chest tightens with anxiety. My hands dig into the armrests even though my gun is burning in my waistband, begging me to take it out. I won't though. I need Gabriel's help. If for nothing more than to make sure I can leave here without a tail and get Olivia safely back home. "Stone received information," I start and then readjust in my seat, exhaling deeply. "Information that implicates me as a cop."

Gabriel clucks his tongue. "Do you know when and how he received that information?"

I'm caught off-guard by the question, but I take a moment and then answer him honestly. "A little over two months ago, one of his men was discovered to be an undercover cop and at some point, information that linked the two of us together also pointed to me being a cop."

"I could see how that would be a serious problem." He presses his lips into a thin straight line. "He knew you were here, and yet he said nothing to me." I nod my head once. It was only discovered two days ago, but it was confirmed tonight. "And you are in fact a cop?"

I hold his gaze and nod once. My heart slams against my chest.

"She isn't. She's innocent." I'm quick to remind him that she has nothing to do with this.

"Of course she is. And I'll make sure we get her home since that's what you want."

A small bit of gratitude washes through me. My angel is safe.He leans forward and squares his shoulders and asks, "What else do you want, Kade?"

I shake my head and I take in a short breath. Once she's safe, I don't know what I can do. Gates told me to abort two days ago. But I couldn't leave yet, not if the report was false. I couldn't waste this chance..

Intel was collected between Ricky and Vic. They were planning my execution. Two days later and the only plan I have now is to get her home safe. Beyond that, I abort or I'm dead. I can't let that man live though. There has to be some justice, no matter how small. I can't leave and do nothing. "I like you, Kade. I've always had a weak spot for you. When I found out about your friend, I hurt for you. I still do." My blood chills at his confession. My brow furrows and then my grip tightens on the armrests. He lowers his eyes to something on his desk and fiddles with it, but I can't tell what it is.

"You knew?" I wasn't told anyone else knew. As far as the department knows, it was only a conversation between Ricky and Vic. And now Vic is dead.

"Of course," Gabriel answers easily. "It's my job to know who's walking through those doors." He clears his throat. "I almost killed you on day one." He holds up his hand and says, "No offense, Kade. I was just doing my job. But then I thought, maybe I could form a much-needed *partnership*. After all, you being a cop means that Ricky is your enemy, too."

"I'm listening." Although my heart hurts at the memory of James, hope fills my chest. We have a common enemy, and that can only work in my favor.

"Do you know who I don't like?" he asks me with a glint in his eyes. "I don't like Ricardo Stone. I don't like what he does, and I don't like how I'm inherently associated with him."

"I can understand how that would reflect poorly." I keep my voice even and wait for him to continue.

"I'd like him to die, Kade."

I nod my head once, relief flowing through me for the first time since I stepped into this office.

"His business is bad for my business. I want him dead, and I want all of his business gone. If that means I have to deal with you," he points his finger at me and then holds it in the air, "one last time before we part ways with no ill feelings, I think that can be arranged."

"What deal are you offering?" I ask him. I don't have anything to bargain with, but I need to know the terms if I'm going to make a deal with the devil.

He gives me an asymmetrical grin and says, "I have enough information on his contacts and operations that if they were to get into the wrong hands, *or the right hands*, well it would do me well to see that happen." Gabriel smiles at me and relaxes in his seat. "He dies, and everyone in this business knows that you did it and I had nothing to do with it." He holds my gaze. "And the information I give to you, you got from him."

"Is that all?" I ask. For the first time in years, I feel like I've made progress in this case. I'm focused on revenge and finally ending this.

"That, and the fact you've never met me or my Talia. You've never been here, and you don't know what they're talking about." He leans back in his seat. "I want this to be a win, win, win for me, Kade. If you make that happen, we'll part dear friends." He gives me a wide smile and says, "In fact, I'll owe you one."

"I'll make sure it happens," I say. I'm eager to accept his deal and finally see a way out of this. But first I need Olivia away from all this. I need her safe. For all I know, Stone will kill me before I can kill him.

Or Gabriel will, once I've done his dirty work for him.

CHAPTER 28

Olivia

"I'M SORRY, ANGEL." I THINK I HEAR KADE'S voice, but my eyelids are so heavy. I feel his small kiss on my forehead. I try to get up so I can kneel for him, but my body doesn't quite respond. I moan out for him, but they aren't the words I want. My head falls to the side.

"It'll wear off soon." I hear his voice, but I don't understand.

"I promise you, I'll keep you safe." I can feel his body

carry me away, but I don't know where to. I can feel a cold breeze on my face, and the sounds of car doors opening.

Outside? Are we leaving? I try to ask, but I can't.

Kade sets me down against leather, and the sounds of a car starting make me realize we are leaving. I want to ask where, but I can't.

I try to roll my body and ask him, but I'm so heavy.

His hand cups my face and he kisses me. His comforting touch puts me at ease.

"Sleep, angel," I hear him say. I'd nod my head if I could. I want to sleep. My body's so tired.

As I drift off into a deep sleep, I swear I hear him say, "Forgive me, angel," and even softer, "I love you."

But I'm not certain of anything. It all feels like a dream.

❄ ❄ ❄

My body stirs with the need to wake up. I've been asleep too long.

Beep. Beep. Beep.

Ugh. My head hurts so much.

I try to lift my body off this hard mattress, but my body is sore and the bright lights make me wince. *Beep. Beep. Beep.*

What is that noise? My head's killing me.

I slowly open my eyes and my body tenses. What the fuck? I'm in a hospital room.

"Kade!" I call out as I bolt upright in the seat.

My head's so dizzy I nearly fall back. I grip onto the cold steel bars on either side of the bed to steady myself. A nurse rushes in through the door, followed by another.

"Miss, please, lie back." She puts her hands on mine and I look around the room as she lays me back against the bed. I don't fight her, but I'm scared. What the fuck am I doing in a hospital?

"Where am I?" I ask her as easily as I can.

"You're at Union Hospital. You were admitted early this morning." My heart beats faster as I try to recall what happened. But I don't know. I don't understand.

"You had some drugs in your system, including rufilin. Can you tell me if you recall anything about last night?"

My body tenses as I shake my head. I don't understand what's going on.

"I don't," I say as I stare at the back wall.

Is this my freedom? He drugged me and left me at a hospital? Is he gone? Tears prick my eyes. He didn't even say goodbye.

I begged him to leave, but I didn't want this. This hurts. My heart literally hurts.

The nurse pulls up a stool next to the bed as the other gives me a small smile and closes the door behind her. She seems less anxious now that I'm not trying to escape.

"We were able to identify you from your license that was in your pocket, but could you tell me your name?"

"Olivia Bell." My voice is even and low. I feel distant. *He left me.* That's all I can think.

She nods her head and places her hand over mine. I can see sympathy in her eyes.

"You've been missing for quite a while."

Her hand pats mine.

"Can you tell me what happened?" she asks in a sweet voice.

I stare at her, not trusting myself to speak.

He left me. The last thing I remember is him pulling my back into his chest. He held my hand and kissed my neck. And then... he had to go? I don't remember. It's so fuzzy. I can't remember.

"I—" I swallow thickly, but I can't speak. I shake my head.

"It's okay," she says, and there's nothing but sympathy in her eyes.

"A missing person's report was filed. The police will be here soon."

I don't want to see them.

"I need a minute, please." I barely get the words out.

She taps my hand and gives me a sad smile. "We'll be right outside. Just press this button if you need anything."

I nod my head and wipe the tears from under my eyes I didn't even realize had escaped.

After a long time, reality slowly registers.

My throat closes and I cover my face as I lose all composure.

I don't stop crying until I hear a knock on the door and the police walk in.

CHAPTER 29

Kade

I'M WALKING INTO A SETUP, AND I KNOW IT. I have nothing to lose though.

I've got a vest on and three guns on me. I'm going with the one with the silencer first.

I shut the door to the car and take a look over my shoulder.

Gabriel and Andrew are parked across the lot at a café. They know it's going down. My heart beats chaotically in my chest, trying to escape. Andrew is Gabriel's right-hand man. He doesn't know everything, but he knows enough. I saw the surprise in his eyes though. I felt like a traitor.

It'll be worth it after today though.Gabriel may kill me the second I walk out of those doors. *If* I walk out. But if he gives me the paperwork and I can pull this off, everything will be worth it.

I could've called my handler, Gates. I could've been pulled. But I keep thinking about James and Olivia. If I leave now, it was all for nothing. His death and everything I put her through would be meaningless. Gabriel won't give me the papers until Stone is dead. This has to happen.

Gates wanted me out when he called. He said we had to abort. My boots crunch on the gravel as I walk up to the old packaging center. Ricky bought it for cheap, and his office is in the back.

No fucking way. Not after Gabriel offered me this deal. If he's telling me the truth.

She's safe. And that's what matters.

I push open the double doors and take a look around. A few men are playing cards on a cheap table to my right. One's smoking some skunked pot, and the scent fills my lungs.

I don't know who all knows I'm undercover. Intelligence says it's just Ricky. So I'm taking my chances. But it could be all of them. I nod at the men and they give me a nod back, and one even a quick wave.

I hope I'm right. I walk down the hall and all the way to the back. With each step my heart beats louder and louder knowing I'm walking to my death... unless I kill him first.

Being back here reminds me of what happened that night.

I thought about it the entire drive back up here. What would've happened if she'd never walked down that alley? I never would have met her. I never would have ruined something so beautiful. But I also wouldn't have gone to Gabriel. She's a bigger part of this than she'll ever know.

I stop in front of the closed door to his office and hesitate before knocking. I could still run. I could leave and never look back.

But I have to do this. I knock on the door twice with the back of my hand. *Knock. Knock.*

I can feel the sweat on my brow and I wipe it away as I hear him say, "Come in."

I take a deep breath and turn the knob. It opens slowly with a creak, and Ricky's right where he always is, smoking a cigarette behind the old desk. I take a quick glance around the room. No one else is here. I shut the door with a loud click and look at the man who thinks he's about to kill me.

"Have a seat, Maddox." The way he says my last name

makes me want to cringe. It's like he's poking fun at it. He knows that's not my real name. Barrow's my real last name. How many times has he done that? How many times has it slipped by me?

I take a seat across from him and let the leather jacket I'm wearing slide up some as I sit back. My hands slip into my pockets, but the right one has a hole at the bottom. My hand slides through and I grip the butt of my gun.

My finger rests on the trigger.

"Kade, I have a few problems with the order coming up." Ricky leans back in his seat, his fingers in a steeple and taps his pointer fingers against his lips.

"We need virgins. They get the good money." I keep my eyes on his and nod.

"These used up cunts aren't bringing in what they used to." Every word that comes from his mouth disgusts me more and more.

"Did you see Vic yesterday?" he asks me. "He's supposed to be on the lookout for buyers, but he hasn't gotten back to me since he was on his way to you."

I play it off smoothly and say, "Didn't see him yesterday. Maybe I left a little too soon." He doesn't believe me. But it doesn't matter.

He leans forward and I follow suit, pulling the gun out slowly.

"Well, I'm gonna need two men to round up the product,

now that that fucker, what was his name?" he asks me with his eyes narrowed.

"Who's that?" I ask him. My heart beats faster. *James.* I know that's who he's talking about.

He gives me a wicked smile as he nods his head and snaps his fingers. "That's right," he says as he pulls out a drawer to his desk.

My heartbeat slows and I pull the gun out. The metal slips against the leather, but I'm quick and efficient. Aim. Fire. Two shots. Both to the head.

The silencer is barely heard as his body jolts with each shot and he falls back in the chair, sagging with two neat bullet holes dripping blood down his face. And the gun he'd picked up from the drawer falls to the thin-carpeted floor with a low thud.

I push back in the chair and it topples over. Done. That fucker's dead. It's about time. If I die right now, at least I contributed some good to the world. I've sure as shit done my fair share of bad. But I'm done.

My heart beats rapidly and adrenaline surges in me as I leave the office, locking the door from the inside and closing it tight.

I walk out as casually as possible, waving goodbye to the fuckers playing cards and walk across the lot to my car.

Gabriel's standing outside the driver's door and as I unlock the car, he opens it for me.

"It's done?" he asks. I nod my head.

"He's dead. Two bullets to the head."

Gabriel smiles and hands me a large manila envelope.

"I don't believe we'll ever see each other again."

"I don't think we will." I answer him with the same tone as I slide into the driver's seat and start the car. I make sure to do it while he's there, just in case. He closes the door and takes in a deep breath as I put the car into reverse.

I place the envelope on the passenger seat. I don't know what's in it, but I don't plan on looking until I get to the safe house.

"It's been fun, Kade. I'm sad to see you go, but I think it's for the best for both of us."

Again I nod. And I have to agree.

Our heads whip around to the packaging center as I hear a dim scream of anger and then another. They found him.

"Time to go," Gabriel says with a smile. "Best of luck to you, Kade."

"Same to you." We lock eyes before parting ways. As I drive out of the lot, I see Andrew give me a short wave from his truck across the road. I return the gesture and drive off. I'm still waiting for a bomb or a bullet.

I anticipate my death the entire three-hour drive to the safe house.

It doesn't hit me until I get there and park and look

through all the documents that Gabriel handed to me, that it's finally over. It's really over.

Every contact, first and last name, alias and locations are all in neat, organized columns.

I lean back in my seat and rest my head against the cold window. It's over.

The hurt and hollowness in my chest doesn't move, and I stay in the car longer than I should before I gather the strength to go in and call Gates. I'll take pictures of the evidence and send them to him... just in case.

I get out of the car slowly and follow through with the orders Gates gave me days ago.

I sit at the desk in the back room and dial the number.

The phone rings and rings.

Finally, a man answers.

I give him the code words, and it's done.

My mission is done.

The only thing I want to do is to run to Olivia. I need to know if she's okay. I need to make sure she's alright. But I could never do that.

The world I've been living in vanishes before my eyes. The reality sets in.

Everything I did to her plays through my mind in slow motion.

I fell in love with her, but she should hate me for what I've done.

CHAPTER 30

Olivia

I LOOK OVER AT CHERYL HESITANTLY. I'VE BEEN home for a few days now. But I haven't left my room much. I haven't talked to my parents. They keep telling me they'll be there when I'm ready. But I don't see how I could ever be ready.

"Just talk to me," Cheryl says and reaches her hand out to me. I want to tell them all, but I know what they'll say. I confessed everything to the shrinks at the hospital and they gave me a pill and said I was sick. I'm not sick. I'm heartbroken; there's a difference.

I don't need anyone else talking to me about Stockholm syndrome. I'm thinking clearly, and functioning just fine. But I miss him. It hurts me so much to not know if he's okay.

It's almost like it never happened. Like I imagined it.

One day I was taken, and two months later I'm dropped off at a hospital. They filed a report even though I told them not to. Doctor-patient confidentiality apparently doesn't mean shit if my state of mind is unwell.

I didn't tell the police anything. I don't want to confide in anyone. I just want Kade back. I rub my chest where the pain is.

"I know they hurt you," Cheryl says and her voice cracks. She just wants me to talk, I know that. But I can't.

"Please don't." I shake my head and stop her right in her tracks. Tears prick my eyes. "Don't." I don't want to hear it. I don't want her pity. I don't want to know what they think happened to me. I know what they think, and I know what they'll say if they ever found out the truth.

"Tell me to do something then. Please." Cheryl's voice is full of desperation. "I feel so guilty." She takes in a ragged breath. "You have no idea. I love you so fucking much, and when you didn't come home I knew something was wrong."

Hot tears run down her cheeks. "I shouldn't have let

you go there alone." She doesn't bother to wipe them away. It was just to an interview. I don't blame her in the least.

I hug her, making the bed bounce slightly. I tighten my arms around her to show her how much I love her. "It's not your fault. It's okay." She holds me back and doesn't let go as a violent sob is ripped from her throat.

"It's not okay." She pulls away from me and angrily wipes the tears. "You're not okay." I barely make out her words through the sobs.

She struggles to even her breathing. She's right; I'm not okay. I don't know if I'll ever be okay. I've never hurt this much before.

I feel abandoned and alone. Even though I'm surrounded by friends who are here for me. I don't want them though. I want Kade.

I take in a steadying breath and prepare to answer her, but a sturdy knock at my door stops me.

"Olivia?" My father's voice is uncertain.

"Yes?" I answer hesitantly.

"There are police officers here to see you." My blood turns to ice, and my body numbs.

I won't talk. I don't want to.

I look down at my body. I'm only in sweats and an old t-shirt. My pajamas basically. I've been wearing the same ones for two days now. They're clean at least. I don't have a bra on though.

"I'll be down in a minute," I answer loud enough for him to hear.

Cheryl's composing herself and wiping her nose with her sleeve as I open the dresser drawer and pull out a bra. Then I open the drawer below it looking for a nicer looking shirt. I turn my back to her to change clothes as quick as I can.

"Are you okay?" Cheryl asks.

I turn, slipping the shirt down and stare at my best friend.

"Are you going to be in trouble? Is that why...?" She doesn't finish, but she doesn't have to.

"No," I say and shake my head.

"What can I do to help?" Her wide eyes, glassy with tears, are pleading with me.

I hold my hand out to her. "I could use a friend." She's quick to take my hand and she doesn't let go as I walk through the hall and down the stairs.

My heartbeat seems to slow with each step and finally I'm in my dining room where an officer in uniform is sitting with my parents at the table and another officer is standing behind him.

"Olivia Bell?" the officer asks.

I clear my dry throat and try to answer, but it's so hard. It feels as though a lump is lodged in it, so I just nod instead.

"I'm Detective Dowers, and this is my partner, Detective Brown."

"Hi," I manage to squeak out.

"We have a few questions for you," the man standing asks. Detective Dowers' nearly bald head reflects the light hanging above the table. His eyes are a soft hazel, but they seem kind.

I nod my head again and pull out a seat, sitting across from the other officer. He's younger, but he looks tired with bags under his eyes.

His voice is deeper, too. "Do you know this man?" He sets a picture down on the table and everyone else in the room takes a look.

My heart stops beating. It's Kade. He's staring back at me. His power is reaching me through his picture.

Life seems to drain from me. I look into the officer's eyes, but I don't answer.

After a moment, he speaks. "We have reason to believe that he abducted you on September 16th."

"Is this the man?" my mother asks as she grips my shoulders and tries to look me in the eyes. But I don't move, I don't react. I feel trapped. I don't know how they found out, but I'm not saying a word. I refuse to say anything against him.

I won't do it.

"Miss?" Everyone's eyes are on me as I lick my dry lips and shake my head no.

"He admitted to kidnapping you."

My eyes flash to Detective Dowers. My heart races, and my blood heats.

"I need to ask you some questions. And you need to answer them truthfully." I slowly move my eyes to Detective Brown as he speaks.

"Olivia. Are you okay?" my mother asks.

"Olivia, you don't need to answer anything," Cheryl's quick to add. She looks up at the officers and says, "She has the right to a lawyer."

"We have no intention of pressing charges against Olivia. She's the victim here."

"What happened?" my father asks. And Detective Dowers looks more than ready to divulge information.

I don't speak as the two officers rattle off the last two months of my life as though it's a series of crimes. They have names and dates. They mention rape and sex slavery. All the while, my parents cry. Even my father.

I sit there numb, listening to it as everyone around me breaks down into hysterics. It's odd to hear what they think of it. Some facts I know could have only come from Kade.

He abandoned me, and then admitted to everything. I wish he'd told me. I would have never let him do it. I feel so betrayed by him. I'm sick to my stomach.

"We need you to answer these questions. And you're going to have to testify."

"What if she doesn't want to face him?!" Cheryl cries out with horror. She hasn't let go of my hand.

"I won't do it." I speak for the first time.

The officers stare at me for a long time.

"We're going to need you to speak to our psychologist." I shake my head. That's not happening either. No fucking way.

"If you refuse," Dowers looks at Brown and sighs as if he's burdened to tell me, "we will subpoena you. And if you fail to follow through with your obligations, charges will be pressed."

"How dare you!" my mother hisses across the table.

"Get out of my house." My father's voice booms through the room. My body shakes, and tears leak from the corner of my eyes.

"I'm very sorry for what's happened to you, but we won't allow you to compromise this case. We will prosecute you to the full extent of the law if you fail to cooperate."

❊ ❊ ❊

That threat has echoed in my head every night for the past two weeks.

Each appointment, every interview.

And now as I get ready to testify against the man I love.

CHAPTER 31

Olivia

"MISS BELL, I ASKED YOU A QUESTION." THE old man distracts me from my thoughts. He stares at me through his glasses, waiting for an answer that I don't want to give him.

"I've told you everything." I feel sick to my stomach. I've answered every question they've thrown at me with complete honesty. Because Kade told me to.

The second I sat down, I'd planned to plead the fifth

and not give them anything against him. But my eyes caught Kade's, and he mouthed to me to tell the truth. I've looked at him every time before answering. And every time he's given me an approving small smile and a nod.

"You've told us about many things, but you have not answered a simple question." The lawyer faces the jury and then looks back to me. "Did this man, Kade Barrow, or Kade Maddox as you knew him, did he or did he not take you against your will on the night of the 16th?" His voice is sharp. He takes his glasses off and purses his lips as he waits for me to answer.

"You don't understand—" I keep trying to explain it to them, but they aren't listening. Knowing now what he did... he saved me. I was in the wrong place at the wrong time. He did what he thought was best. And he kept me safe.

"I understand this man held you captive, and that you are suffering because of it. This man is withholding information on a Gabriel Durand. He's murdered his own partner in cold blood. He's committed crime after crime, and you've testified to those facts." His cold eyes bore into me as he asks, "Have you not?"

Tears prick my eyes and my heart squeezes with unbearable pain. I only did it because he told me to. Tears flow freely down my cheeks. I look back at Kade. He gives me a soft smile, and it breaks my heart. A sob is ripped from my throat.

"Yes," I answer barely above a murmur.

The man looks between me and Kade with disgust.

"No further questions, your Honor."

❖ ❖ ❖

I grip onto the edge of my dress and hold my breath as I listen to the judge deliver his sentencing.

The hearing continues in a daze, as if it isn't real.

"How do you find the defendant?" the judge asks.

The clerk looks straight ahead as he answers, "The jury finds the defendant guilty."

My stomach sinks and churns with a sickness threatening to come up. The words sink in slowly, and my grip loosens. My lungs empty and refuse to fill.

The judge nods his head and addresses Kade. "Kade Barrow, although you engaged in activity you felt was required while you were acting on behalf of the police force, you've testified to several illegal activities that were in clear and direct violation of the law. You refused a direct order to abort, and therefore you will not be able to hide behind the guise of an officer of the law."

My ears fill with white noise and my vision goes black. My hands and body chill with a numbness as the judge sentences Kade to fifty years in prison.

Soft murmurs fill the courtroom, but I'm silent, refusing to believe what's happening.

"The jury is thanked and excused. Court is adjourned."

The gavel slams down hard with a loud bang and people stand around me. They're going to get up and do whatever it is that's waiting for them.

I stare at the back of Kade's head, waiting for him to look at me.

But he doesn't. He stands and walks behind the bailiff. He never turns.

My throat closes and my face heats.

A door opens to the left of the judge's bench for them to walk through.

I just need one look from him. Just one sign that I mean anything to him. I need to know it was real between us. That I'm not crazy.

But they walk through the door and it closes behind them without him ever looking back at me.

I collapse forward and cover my face with my hands. I don't care that they can see me. I don't care who hears me. I break down like I never have before. My heart is beyond broken, it's shattered.

CHAPTER 32

Kade

THIS ISN'T THE FIRST TIME I'VE BEEN GIVEN this offer.

I stare down at the sheet I'm about to sign. But I can't even wrap my head around it. I can only think about her. It's been ten days since the hearing, and every day I'm filled with regret.

I needed to do it for her though. I thought I was going away for fifty years. I couldn't let her even consider waiting for me. She would have, my sweet angel. I know she would have. And I don't want that life for her. She deserves a man who will be there for her, someone to give her children and a life worth living. With this deal, I can be that man for her. It'll be a few years. But I can give her that, if she'll wait for me. If she wants me.

"You aren't promising millions of dollars this time though, so maybe it's more believable," I say without any humor in my voice as I tap the pen against the table.

"You'll be heavily compensated for your enrollment in the program," the man in the suit, Mr. Smith, says. A Mr. Thomas was the one who offered me and James the deal that got me into this shit.

"It's three years overseas, or fifty years in jail." Mr. Smith stands up from the table, straightening out his tie. "Your choice."

❖ ❖ ❖

I leave tomorrow. A plane's going to take me to Nepal and then god knows where else. For the next three years of my life, I'll be doing the government's bidding. Making up for my past crimes.

"We're here," the taxi driver says. I'm quick to get out and pull out my wallet.

I pay the tab, giving him an extra ten in cash and turn to look at the building.

It's her house.

I have one night of freedom. They gave me a single night, and I came straight here.

I never told her how I felt. I didn't get a chance to explain anything. I shove my hand in my pocket and feel the note I wrote her.

It's an apology for everything I've done.

A confession of how I feel about her.

And a promise to come back.

I walk slowly up the steps, my confidence slipping as I get closer. I don't know that she'll want me, but I have to tell her everything.

I hear her small voice as I come up to the front porch.

There's a porch swing and a huge window behind it. The window's open, and the thin curtains don't do anything to obstruct my view. I can see right inside. My eyes focus on her.

The beast that's been pacing inside of me since the hearing settles when I see her, my angel. She has a way about her that does that to me. She tames and calms me.

She looks beautiful in simple grey sweats and a pale pink tank top. Her ankles are crossed as she sits at a dining room table. Her hair's in a loose bun on top of her head.

She looks so relaxed and at home. She looks... normal. My heart speeds up as she turns to the window. I move out of sight as fast as I can, afraid she saw me. But she doesn't say anything.

"It's going to be alright, Olivia. We're here to help you," a woman's voice says. That must be her mother.

Olivia clears her throat as I peek back inside. I finally get a look at her face. She's so sad. She has bags under her eyes, and her lips are turned down. She's not okay.

"You don't understand," she says quietly.

"Well, tell me then. Please." Her mother's voice cracks and she sniffles, picking up a napkin to wipe under her eyes. My heart shatters in my chest. I'm feeling like a million splinters are stabbing me in every direction. This is my fault.

"You don't tell any of us anything." Her father's voice is hard.

"Harold, stop it," her mother snaps. "She'll tell us when she's ready."

Olivia's quiet. She doesn't respond. She sets her fork down and pushes the plate away.

"You need to eat, baby." Her father's voice is low and non-threatening.

They care about her. They're trying to help her. They're going to heal her when I can't.

Heal her pain that I caused.

I close my eyes and clench my fists.

What the fuck am I even doing here? I did this to her.

I crumple the note in my pocket and lower my head. I watch my feet move as I walk through the yard and down the empty street. There aren't any street lights. It's dark and lonely. It's what I deserve.

She deserves so much more than me. She deserves the life she would've had without me.

It's wrong of me to even ask for forgiveness.

I was in too deep. I refused to leave when I should have.

I'll do what I should have done from the beginning. I'll leave her alone. She's better off without me.

CHAPTER 33

Olivia

Three years later...

I CAN'T STOP SMILING. I ROCK BACK AND FORTH
on my heels on the stage as the crowd claps and cheers. I
hold my diploma tighter, feeling nearly unstoppable.

I have my degree in business and a dream job at a winery that I'll hopefully be able to take over soon. I can't believe how quickly life has changed for me.

I look out into the crowd, but no one's there for me right now. My parents' flight is delayed, and I haven't talked to Cheryl since I moved all the way out to California. Well, not like we used to. In all honesty, none of them ever understood why I felt that way about Kade. They never will, and that's okay.

"Are you ready?" Gwen squeals in my ear as we walk off the stage.

"Fuck yeah I am." I smile back at her and start to feel the excitement of being free from school. I've buried myself in work since I've started this journey of recovery. Inwardly I roll my eyes.

My heart was broken. It was shattered. But I'm okay now. I still miss him though. I can't help that. Some things stick with us forever, and Kade and our time together is something I'm choosing not to let go of. I know he's gone. He never loved me like I loved him. If he did, he never told me. I still dream that he did. Sometimes I remember his touch and I question whether or not I'm exaggerating it.

"Are you actually going to try to score tonight?" Gwen grips my hand and pulls me through the crowd. As if by the time we get to the parking lot it's not going to be packed. There are hundreds of cars out there, I don't see the point in rushing just to sit in traffic, but whatever floats her boat I guess.

"One sec," I say and pull back on her hand so I can slip off my heels. She scrunches her nose and I respond by sticking my tongue out.

"At least you'll go faster," she says.

I smirk at her. "Precisely!"

❖ ❖ ❖

I sway my hips to the beat of the music booming through the club. I slowly raise my arms with a drink in my right hand. It's dark, but the lights flash every few beats and the up lighting gives the club a hot vibe I've grown to love. This is our place to unwind. And I enjoy every minute of it. I like getting lost in the seductive beats.

Gwen bumps her ass into me and shakes it while sticking her tongue out, making me laugh. I look around, wondering who she's putting a show on for.

I don't see anyone staring back, so I smack her ass playfully and let out a laugh. I'm definitely buzzed and enjoying this night. I start work in one week, and I've gotta pack my shit up, move and get settled. I don't have much, but it's going to keep me busy. Tonight I can just enjoy myself though. I can have a little fun and take in the moment.

Gwen stands upright and turns to face me, mimicking my movements. She leans forward, unsteady on her heels. I quickly balance her, grabbing onto her arm and we both laugh. It's getting late and I think she's had more than enough to drink. I've had my fair share, and my feet are killing me. I'm more than happy to call it a night.

"Wanna go?" I ask her, practically screaming so she can hear me over the booming music.

"But Mr. McHotStuff saw!" she screams in my ear.

"Who?" I scrunch my forehead and look through the crowd as she points behind me. My heart stops in my chest, and my skin chills as I see him.

"He's all yours, baby! He hasn't taken his eyes off of you." I barely hear her voice.

Kade.

I stare back at him, not knowing what to do. I'm afraid to move, afraid to breathe even. I've thought I'd seen him a hundred times before, but it was never him.

I'm afraid if I blink, he'll vanish.

"Kade?" I whisper. And as though I've broken the spell, he turns and pushes through the crowd, leaving me.

Gwen grips onto my arm as I try to leave. "Where are you going?" she screams over the music with a worried look in her eyes.

I shake my head at her and point to the bar. "I'll meet you there in ten."

She points her finger at me. "Ten minutes."

I'd laugh at her trying to be the responsible one if I had any humor in me, but I don't. My blood pumps with adrenaline and anxiety as I push past the swaying hips on the dance floor and search for Kade.

I make it through the crowd and out to the other side in

time to see Kade looking back over his shoulder and walking through the exit door.

I don't even hesitate. I'm not letting him get away from me.

I practically run in my heels to catch the door before it closes and yell out, "Kade!" as I see his back.

There are a few people out here smoking by the door. I barely notice them even though they stopped talking the moment I yelled. I'm sure they're staring, but I don't care.

Kade stops walking, but he doesn't turn around.

I take a few hesitant steps toward him but stay a few feet away. It's late and dark, but there are lights out here on the sides of the building. I can hear the low music get louder as the back door opens and then it dims as the door shuts with a loud click.

It's almost silent, save the sounds of the cars on the street at the end of the alley and the faint beat of the bass from inside the club.

"Kade?" I weakly call out to him. "Please," I start to beg him, but my throat closes and tears prick my eyes. I'd give anything to be with him. But he left as soon as he saw me. Nothing's changed. He doesn't want to be with me.

"You never loved me, did you?" I talk to his back, but that finally gets a reaction from him. He turns around, and my heart slows.

He still looks the same.

His sharp jaw has several days of stubble and his hair is grown out slightly, but the dominance and hard features are still present and they make me want to drop to my knees in this dirty alley. But I don't. I won't do that for a man who doesn't love me.

He opens his mouth, but doesn't say anything. He swallows thickly and watches the door as it opens, bringing the loud noises of the club along with it. He closes the space between us and puts his hand on my hip, although his eyes are on whoever left the building. I can hear their steps grow distant as they walk in the opposite direction and farther away from us.

Finally, he looks down into my eyes.

My heart clenches in my chest. I don't know why he's here; he's supposed to be in jail. I tried so hard to track him down that first year. But they wouldn't tell me anything. I felt pathetic for even trying to find him, but also like I'd failed him for never seeing him. But then again, I found solace knowing he'd never looked back.

In this moment, I know one of two things will happen. Either he tells me he loves me and we find a way to make this work between us, or he doesn't and I leave him behind forever.

"I just need to know if you ever loved me." I stare into

his eyes and ignore the tears running down my face. It may kill a small part of me to hear he never did, but I'll survive. I just need to know.

He cups my jaw in his hand and runs his thumb along my bottom lip. My head falls back slightly and my lips part.

"I should tell you I never did. I should do that for you. I should lie." Hope blooms in my chest, and I take in a deep breath.

"But I'm a selfish man, and I love you so fucking much." My heart swells and hurts so much I can hardly stand it. This time it's a good pain.

"I don't deserve you, and I'll understand it if you send me away. I'll stay away; I promise I will. But if you have any feelings for me left at all, I want you, Olivia. I want to build a life with you. An honest life. I'm done with all that. I promise you."

I wipe the tears away from under my eyes, trying to calm myself, but it's so hard. I've dreamed of him coming back for me, but I never thought it was possible. I didn't think I'd ever see him again.

He loves me.

I want to beat my fists against his chest for leaving me. For throwing me away all those years ago. For not telling me the truth. For never looking back. Somewhere in me, there's anger.

But more than anything, I just want him to hold me. I miss him.

I lose all composure and wrap my arms around him, kissing him with everything I have.

And he holds me back just as tight, kissing me with passion and longing. He pulls my body against his hard, muscular chest. His tongue dives into my mouth and I lean into him. My body lights with a desire I haven't known for years.

He breaks the kiss and pulls away, both of us breathing heavily. "Not here, angel." He kisses my hair and looks back at the door.

After a long moment, I finally ask him, "You're really here?"

"I'm here, Olivia. If you want me, I'm here."

"I do want you."

"Somehow I knew you'd come back for me," I whisper into his chest. I don't know how, but I knew. Years later, I still feel like my heart belongs to him.

"I'm so sorry." He kisses my hair and holds me closer to him. "I wanted you to live your life. I wanted so much more for you than what I could give you. I'll make it up to you. Every day for the rest of my life."

"All I want is you, Kade. I love you." I need him. My heart and soul need him.

"I'm all yours, angel." He pulls away from me and kisses the tip of my nose. "I love you."

EPILOGUE

Olivia

"YOU TWO LOOK SO CUTE TOGETHER! HOW DID you meet?" the waitress asks as we sit down to dinner. She looks sweet and innocent, but I hate it when people ask that question. I hate lying.

In the three years we've lived in the area, I've never been to this restaurant before. I love the seaside cabin feel of it. It's a good hour away from the winery, but I needed a vacation, and Kade said this is the first stop.

The renovations on the winery are seriously eating into its profits, but luckily Kade's investments are paying for this trip. He doesn't understand why I don't just quit since we don't need the money, but I like being challenged and learning the business. Maybe one day I'll sell it, and until then I have his complete support to pursue my dream.

I lay the white cloth napkin across my lap and smooth it out.

"At a club." I give the answer I always give. Kade reaches across the table and takes my hand. He knows I hate this.

"Oh, I love hearing these stories." She hugs the menus to her chest. If only I'd told her the truth.

"I'm starving," I not-so-subtly say to get this conversation moving. Kade chuckles at me and accepts the menu as the waitress hands one to him and then to me.

"You should try not to look so pissed when you answer that question," Kade says as the waitress leaves us.

"Well," I say as I open the menu and look down the list of fresh fish. "Maybe we should come up with a different story." I wouldn't change anything between us. Not a damn thing. But I don't want to share it with anyone. They'll never understand.

Kade brings my hand to his lips and kisses my fingers.

"I don't want another story. I love *our* story." His confession makes my lips kick up into a small smile. "It's sad at times, and we went through hell. But I love you."

Tears prick my eyes. "I love you too, Master K." I blush as I say his name and he raises his brows.

"Don't start what you can't finish, angel." His voice is low and laced with a threat. A threat that makes my pussy clench. We'll be on vacation for days. I've been looking forward to this since I found out we were going.

"I would never." I look up at him through my thick lashes and see nothing but devotion in his eyes. Our story may not be the typical love story, but it's ours, and no one can take that away from us.

Thank you for reading Broken. I hope you loved reading it as much as I loved writing it.

If you haven't already read the first book in the Valetti Crime family series, Dirty Dom (Available Now!), have a little sneak peek:

DIRTY DOM

A BAD BOY MAFIA ROMANCE (VALETTI CRIME FAMILY)

WINTER WILLOWS

Dominic Valetti is only interested in two things: getting paid and getting laid.

He's a bookie for the Valetti crime family, and he knows his sh*t. Dom's busy doing business, no time to dabble in social niceties. The women that chase after him wanting more than a dirty, hard f*ck are only gonna get their hearts broken.

That is, until Becca stumbles into his office to pay off her ex's debt. A hot brunette who's just as guarded as he is and has a body made for sin...and for him. They're not meant to be together. A woman like her shouldn't be with a man like him. He's mobbed up; she's a good girl who deserves better.

When they push their boundaries and cave to temptation, they both forget about the danger. And that's a mistake a man like Dom can't afford. Will Dirty Dom risk it all to keep Becca safe, or will he live up to his name?

This is a standalone, full-length mafia romance with a filthy-mouthed, possessive bad boy. Guaranteed HEA.

PROLOGUE

Dom | Becca

I CRACK MY KNUCKLES AND STRETCH OUT MY arms while **looking out over the football stadium from my suite. I fucking love that this is my office. But then again, when you do what I do, your "office" can be anywhere. I snatch my scotch from the bar and tell Johnny to grab our lunch. Taking a seat on the sectional, I grab my phone to look at my schedule. My first drop off should be here soon.**

—

I'm so fucking nervous. I click my phone on and see I have fifteen minutes to find the bookie's suite. I grab my purse tighter, holding the Coach Hobo closer to my side. I've got 12k in cash under a scarf and the idea that I'm going to be mugged and then killed by the bookie is making my blood rush with adrenaline and anxiety. I can't believe Rick would put me in this position. Shit. I'm such a bitch. I swallow the lump in my throat and square my shoulders to keep the tears pricking the back of my eyes from surfacing. Now is not the time to think about Rick. And it's not like he asked me to do this. His problems keep coming after me and I wanted to cover my bases.

———

The knock at the door seems hesitant and that makes a deep, rough chuckle rumble in my hard chest. Whoever's behind it is scared and I live for that fear. They're right to be scared. I didn't get where I am today by being kind and understanding. Fuck that. I'm a ruthless prick and I know it. My chest hollows for a fraction of a second, but I shut that shit down ASAP. I'm a tough fucker and I'm not going to let some pussy emotions make me weak. Some days I wish I didn't have to be such a cruel asshole. I don't like fucking guys up, breaking their legs and hands or whatever body part they pick – if I let them choose. But they know what they're signing up for when they do business with me. Damn shame they don't have a doctorate

degree in statistics from Stanford, like me. A devilish grin pulls at my lips. If you're gonna be making bets with me, you better be ready to pay up.

—

I wipe the cold sweat from my hands and onto my skirt, ball my small fist tighter and knock on the door a little harder. I wonder if the people walking by know why I'm here. I swallow thickly, feeling like a dirty criminal. My eyes dart to an older woman with kind eyes and grey-speckled hair pushing a caterer's cart. I'm sure she knows. I'm sure everyone who looks at me knows I'm up to no good.

My eyes glance from left to right as I wait impatiently. Sarah's waiting outside and I have to pick up my son from soccer practice soon. I lick my lower lip as the nerves creep up. I'll just pretend this isn't real. Just hand them the money and walk away. Back to real life. Back to my assistant and move on with my normal, non-threatening, everyday life.

—

I take my time getting to the door. No matter how much money they owe me, or how much they've won, they need to know that I do everything whenever the fuck I please. If they have to wait, they have to wait. But I sure as shit don't wait for them. I open the door and my cold, hard heart pumps with hot blood and desire.

A petite woman in fuck-me pink heels and a grey dress that clings to her curves and ends just above her knees is

staring back at me with wide, frightened hazel eyes. Her breasts rise and fall, peeking out of the modest neckline. Her black cardigan is covering up too much of her chest and I barely resist the urge to push it off her shoulders. My eyes travel along her body in obvious appreciation before stopping at her purse. She's clinging to it like it's her life line. My jaw ticks, what's a woman like her doing making bets with a guy like me? Johnny handles most of that shit now. We aren't supposed to take bets from women. I don't like it. I'm definitely going to have to ask him about her.

—

The door opens and I nervously peek up at the gorgeous man looking down at me through my dark, thick lashes. The lines around his eyes means he's every bit the man he looks, but his devilish white-toothed grin gives him a boyish charm meant to fool women like me. He's fucking hot in a black three-piece suit that's obviously tailored to fit his large chiseled frame perfectly. With that crisp, white button-down shirt and simple black tie you'd think he was a young CEO, but his muscular body, piercing blue eyes and messy brunet hair that's long enough to grab, makes him a sex god. Lust and power radiate from his broad chest as his eyes travel down my body. He looks like a man who knows how to destroy you.

A wave of desire shoots through me when my eyes meet his heated stare. My breathing hitches and I swallow down my distress with my treacherous body. I'll just give him the money Rick owed him and get the fuck out of here. At the reminder of why I'm standing in his doorway, I push my purse towards him.

———

I grin at her obvious nervousness and cock a brow, "Purses aren't my style, doll." Pulling the door open wider, I step aside, just enough for her to get through. Her soft body gently brushes mine as she walks through the small opening I gave her. The subtle touch sends a throbbing need to my dick and I feel it harden, pushing against my zipper. She hustles a little quicker when I lean closer to her. Her hips sway and I stifle a groan when I see that dress clinging to her lush ass. Fuck, I want that ass. I never mix business with pleasure, but there's an exception to every rule. Something about her just pulls me in. Something about the way she's carrying herself. Like she needs me, or I need her. My dick jumps as she turns around to fully face me. Fuck, at least one part of me desperately wants her attention.

———

His body touching mine makes every nerve ending in my core ignite; I nervously squeeze the strap of my purse. I just want to get the hell out of here. My stupid heart is longing for comfort. My trembling body is aching with need. What the hell is wrong with me? It's only been three days; I should have more respect for Rick than this. I will the tears to go away. I just want to be held. But I know better. This man staring back at me, he isn't a man who will hold me. I take in a gasp of air and turn around to face the man my husband owed money to while digging in my purse to gather the bundles of cash.

———

"Is it all there?" I have no fucking clue who she is or what she's supposed to be giving me. Johnny has the list, but he's not back yet with our lunch. It's a rarity that I even have to speak during drops. I just like to watch. And when it comes to people not paying up, it's best that I'm here.

———

"I'm sorry it's late." His rough fingers brush mine as I hold out the thick bundle of hundreds. His touch sends a shot of lust to my heated core and I close my eyes, denying the desperate need burning inside me. It would feel so good to let him take me the way a man should. I haven't been touched in months. I haven't felt desire in nearly a year, and I know for a fact, I've never felt such a strong pull to a man, never wanted to give myself to someone like I do him.

———

"What about the interest?" Her eyes widen with fear and her breath stalls as her plump lips part. If it's late,

then she should know to pay that extra 5% per day. Compounded. Johnny should've told her all that shit. But judging by her silence and that scared look on her face, she doesn't have a clue. A grin pulls to my lips, but I stifle it. I want her to think I'm mad. I want her to feel like she owes me. I don't want her money though. She can pay me in a way I've never been paid before. I don't accept ass as payment, but for her, fuck yeah I'll take it.

———

The man on the phone said not to worry about being late. He said he was sorry for my loss and that he understood. I feel my breath coming up short as a lump grows in my throat. Fuck! What the hell am I going to do? Fucking Rick, leaving me with this shit to deal with. I wish I could just fucking hide as these damn tears start pricking my eyes. My hands start to shake as I realize I'm trapped in the bookie's suite and I owe him money.

———

"Aw, doll. Don't cry. We can work something out." Her bottom lip's trembling and her gorgeous hazel eyes are brimming with tears. I feel like a fucking asshole for taking advantage of the situation. But then again, what the fuck did she expect? First, she made a bet with a bookie – not fucking smart on her part. Then she comes late to hand over the dough. She had to know there'd be consequences. She parts her lips to respond, but she's too shaken up. My heart clenches looking at her small frame trembling with worry.

I'll make it good for her. She looks like a girl I could keep. My brows furrow as I reach out to brush her cheek with my hand. I'm not sure where that thought came from, but the more I think about it, the more I like it. She closes her eyes and leans into my touch as I wipe away the tear trailing down her sun-kissed skin. As I reach her lips, I part them with my thumb.

———

I hate the bastard tears that've escaped. I feel too raw and vulnerable. I can't help but to love the warmth of his skin. How long has it been since someone's touched me with kindness and looked at me with desire? I *need* this. I need to be held. If only for a little while. His thumb brushes my bottom lip and I instantly part them for him. He can hold me for a moment. I can pretend it's more. I can pretend he really wants me. I can pretend he loves me.

———

Fuck, she's so damn perfect. Leaning into me like she really wants me. Like she needs me. She radiates sweet innocence, but there's something more about her, something I can't quite put my finger on. A sting of loneliness pulses through me. I was playing with the thought of having her on her knees in exchange for payment. But I want more. I want her to fucking love what I do to her. I'll make her want me when it's over. A coldness sweeps through me. They always want me after, but it's for the money, not for me. A sad smirk plays at my lips as she licks my thumb and massages the underside with her hot tongue. Fuck, I'll take it. If she only wants me for my money, I'll take it. I feel a burning need to keep her.

My brows furrow in anger at my thoughts. My fucking heart is turning me into a little bitch. "Strip. Now." My words come out hard, making her take a hesitant step back as I pull my thumb from her lips. I instantly regret being the fucking asshole I am. But I can't take it back. I turn my back to her, to lock the door. I slip the gun out from under my belt and easily hide it from her sight to set it down on the table by the door. God knows what she'd think if she got a look at it.

—

My body flinches as the hard sound of the door locking echoes through the room. He moves with power and confidence, his gaze like one of a predator. I swallow my pride and slip off my cardigan. I don't need pride and self-respect right now; I need a man to desire me. The thought and his hungry eyes on me has me peeling off my dress without hesitation. I don't care if this is a payment or if he's just using the interest as an excuse to fuck me; I want this. Or at least I want him.

As I reach behind my back to unhook my bra, he reaches for me, wrapping his strong arms around my body and molding his hard chest to mine. His lips crush against mine and I part them for his hot tongue to taste me. He kisses me with passion and need. His hard dick pushes into my stomach. The feeling makes my pussy heat and clench. Yes. The tears stop, but my chest is still in agony. *Make it go away, please. Take my pain away.*

—

She fucking needs me; I can feel it. And I sure as fuck need her. I don't even hesitate to unleash my rigid cock from my pants. I rip her skimpy lace panties from her body, easily shredding them and tossing them to the floor. I squeeze her ass in my hands, pulling her body to mine. I slam her against the wall, keeping my lips to hers the entire time. My chest pounds; hot blood pumps through me. I need to be inside her. I line my dick up with her hot entrance, rubbing my head through her slick pussy lips.

Fuck she wants me just as I want her. I slam in to the hilt. She breaks our kiss to lean her head back, banging it against the wall and screaming out with pleasure as I fuck recklessly into her tight pussy. My right hand roams her body while my left keeps her pinned to the wall. Her arousal leaks from her hot pussy and down to my thighs.

—

My legs wrap tightly around him as he ruts into me

with a primitive need. My body knows I need his touch, my heart needs his lips and it clenches as he gives them to me. He frantically kisses me as he pounds into me with desperation. The position he has me in ensures he pushes against my throbbing clit with each thrust. I feel my body building, every nerve ending on high alert.

His lips trail my neck and he leaves small bites and open-mouthed kisses along my neck, my shoulder, my collar bone. He licks the dip in my throat before trailing his hot tongue up my neck. I moan my pleasure in the cold air above us. My heart stills and my body trembles as a numbness and heat attack my body at once. "Yes!" I scream out as my pussy pulses around his thick cock. My body convulses against his as heat and pleasure race through my heavy limbs. I feel waves of hot cum soak my aching pussy. My eyes widen as the aftershocks settle. What the fuck did I just do? I need to get out of here.

—

She's pushing against me like she can't wait to leave and that makes my damn heart drop in my chest. Fine. It's fine. It's not like this was anything more than a payment. I say that over and over while I turn my back on her to grab my pants. I walk across the suite to grab a tissue for her to clean up from the desk, but when I face her, she's already dressed. My blood runs cold with her dismissal of me and what we just shared. It wasn't just some fuck. There was

something there. I've never felt like that before. I never felt THAT before. Whatever it is. I fucking want it. And I'm a man who gets what he wants. My conviction settles as I stride back to her. I'll have her again. I'll make sure it happens.

———

What the fuck have I done? I need to go. I have to go to my son. I want nothing more than for this man to hold me, but I know that's not going to happen. I'm so fucking stupid. I don't even know his name. These feelings in my fucked up chest aren't the same for him. This was just a payment. The thought makes my heart stop and my chest pain, but I brush it aside. I refuse to be any weaker in front of him. I need to be strong for just a moment longer. I try to fix my hair as best as I can without a mirror. I straighten my back and grab my purse as he walks back over to me.

———

Women like it when I'm an asshole. Don't know why and I don't care, but it always has them coming back to me. I definitely want to see this girl again; I fucking need to be inside her as often as I can. So after I walk her sweet ass to the door I give her a cocky smirk and kiss her cheek.

———

He leans in and whispers against my ear, letting his hot breath tickle my sensitized neck, "Thanks for the payment, doll." With that he turns his back and shuts the door without giving me a second glance. That's the moment the lust-filled hope dies and my heart cracks and crumbles in my hollow chest.

—

I count the money and start pacing. I need her info from Johnny. I need to know who this woman is. Whoever she is, she's going to end up being mine. Not five minutes after she's gone, Johnny comes back. "The first drop just left. She came with everything, but the interest." I pocket her panties so he won't see them. "Twelve grand right?"

"We didn't charge her interest; she didn't know about her husband's debt until yesterday."

"Since when is that how we do business?" I don't even try to keep my voice down. Blood starts pounding in my ears. "Why the fuck is she paying her husband's debt? He doesn't have the balls to come here himself? He sends his woman!" The words jump from my lips before I have a moment to think.

I'm usually more controlled, more thoughtful. If this job has taught me anything it's that silence is deadly and being a hot head will get you killed. But I'm shaking with rage. Anger seeps out of my pores. Anger that she's married to a fucking coward and a bastard. But more than that, I'm fucking pissed that she's taken.

Johnny shakes his head in confusion and slows his movements as he takes in my rage. "No it's not like that. He died last week, heart attack or something."

—

The moment Sarah sees me, the last bit of my hardened exterior cracks. I feel my lips tremble and bite down to prevent the tears. "What did you do, Becca?" Sarah's pleading eyes makes me feel even shittier. She knows, she can tell. I'm sure I look like I just got fucked. My neck is pulsing from where he was biting me.

Her eyes want me to tell her she's wrong, they're begging me to tell her she's mistaken, but I can't lie. I can feel his cum leaking out of me and running down my thigh. Evidence of my weakness and my betrayal. The tears well in my eyes and I can't stop a few from leaving angry, hot trails down my cheeks. All I can manage to reply is the barest of truths, "I slept with him."

"Don't cry Becca. It's alright."

"Rick just died and I slept with a stranger." I don't keep my own disgust out of my voice.

"It's not like you two were even together in the end anyway. You were separated for nearly two months." My breath comes in spasms as I rest my head on the door of my car. I loved my husband, but I can't remember the last time he held me, the last time we made love. A criminal who probably would've hurt me had I shown up empty hand-ed gave me more compassion and desire than Rick has in years.

———

My breath catches in my throat. I took advantage of her in a moment of weakness, but I didn't fucking know how vulnerable she was. I slam my fist against the window. I didn't fucking know! A sick, twisted churning makes me want to heave. Fuck, I treated her like some random slut. She probably thinks I'm a fucking animal for doing that to her. Fuck! I knew she needed me. I fucking knew it.

———

I just needed to be held and feel like I was loved. This shattering in my chest, jagged pieces of glass digging into my heart, it wasn't worth it. It hurts too much. The worst part is that a very large part of me wants, no needs, to crawl back to him and beg him to hold me again. Just one more time.

I wish I hadn't let her go.

I wish I'd never had to meet with him.

I clench my teeth and close my eyes, wondering if I'll ever see her again.

I breathe deep and steady myself to drive away, knowing I'll never see him again.

I hate myself.

I hate myself.

I'm such a dirty bastard.

More by Willow Winters

Join my Naughty List
http://eepurl.com/b2izzf

Get access first to new releases and big giveaways.
Get a FREE Bad Boy Billionaire Romance
just for signing up!

If you'd be interested in getting my latest books
for FREE (and before release!) in exchange for
an honest review, you can also sign up for my
Advance Review Copy Team mailing list here:
http://eepurl.com/b3jNnP

You can check out my Facebook page for sneak peeks
at upcoming books, giveaways, or just to send a
message to my Facebook profile, Willow Winters

And check out my Begging for Bad Boys Facebook
group for ARC invitations, Freebies and New Releases
from your favorite Bad Boy Romance authors.

Or, if all else fails, I check my email often! You can get a
hold of me anytime at:
badboys@willowwinterswrites.com

Made in the USA
Middletown, DE
15 April 2017